FUN WITH POKÉMON!

Art by Hiroshi Takase

What Is Wrong With This Picture?

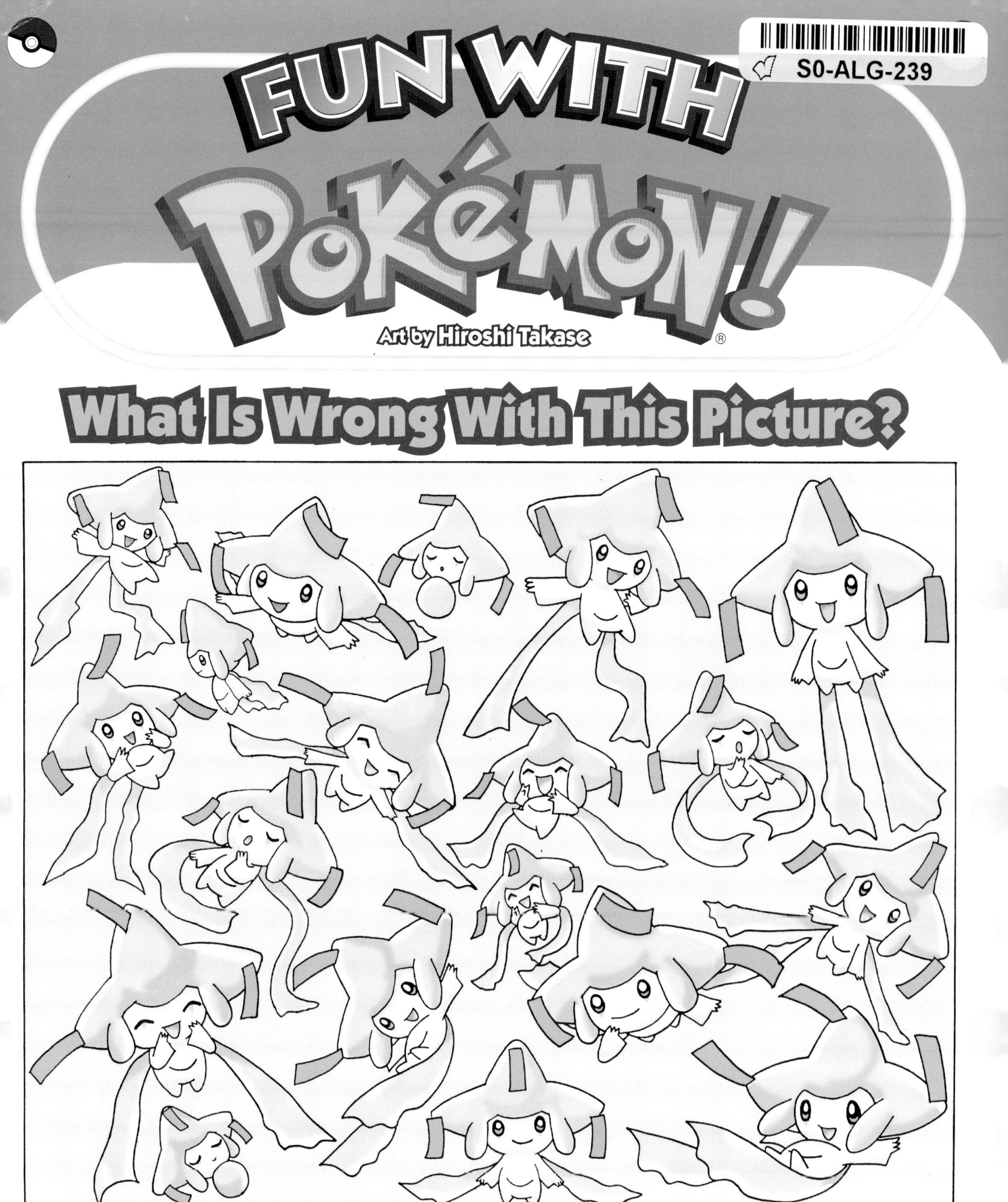

Which Pose Appears Twice?

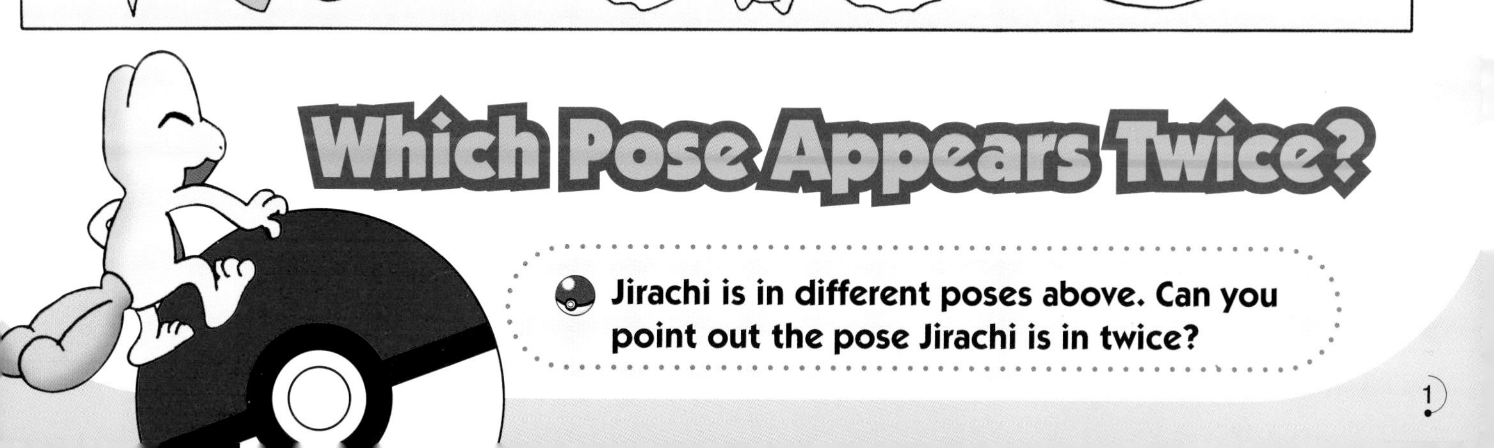

Jirachi is in different poses above. Can you point out the pose Jirachi is in twice?

What Is Wrong With This Picture? 1

Pokémon are playing in the woods.

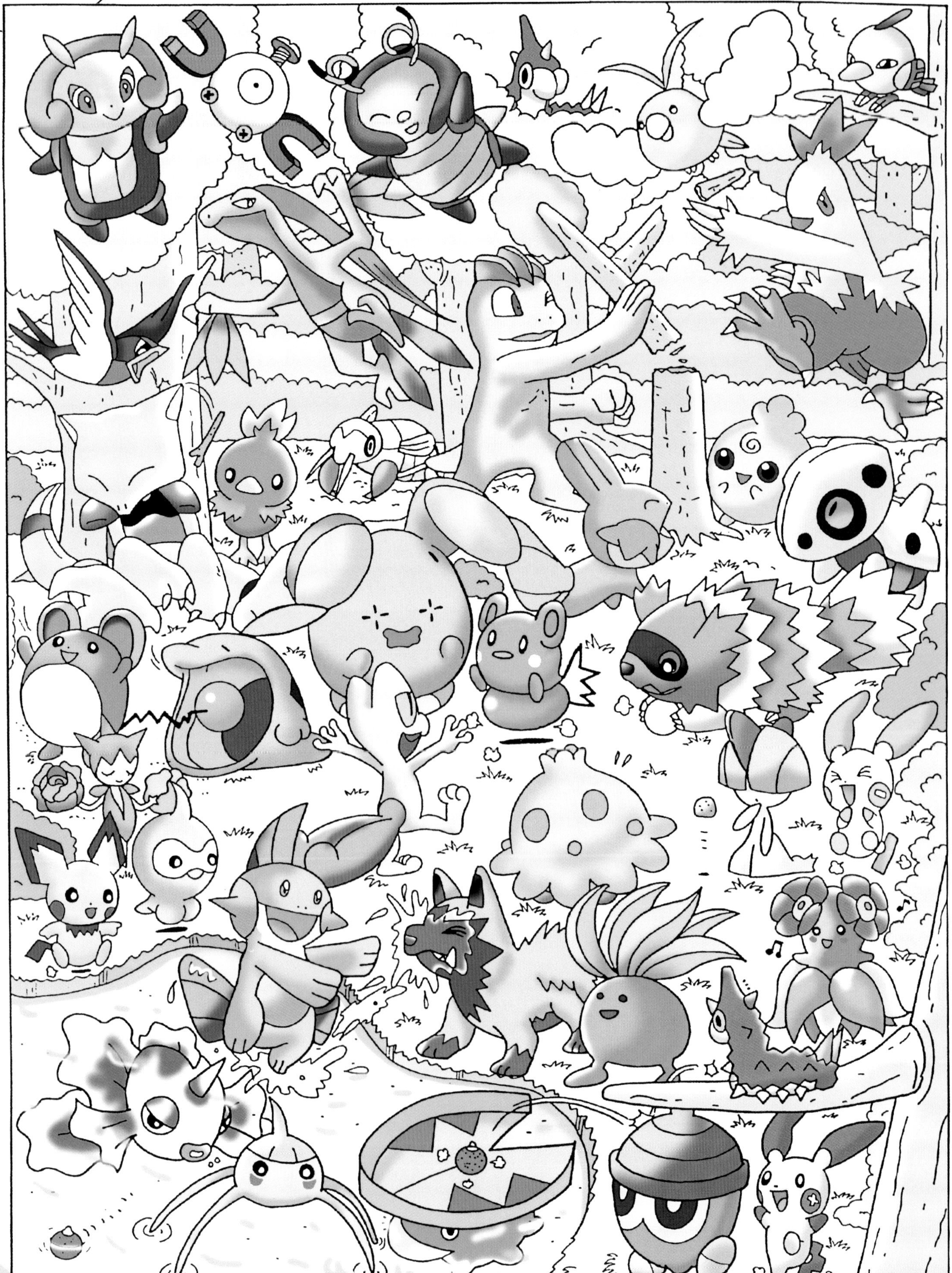

Circle each of the 10 items which do not match the picture on the left.

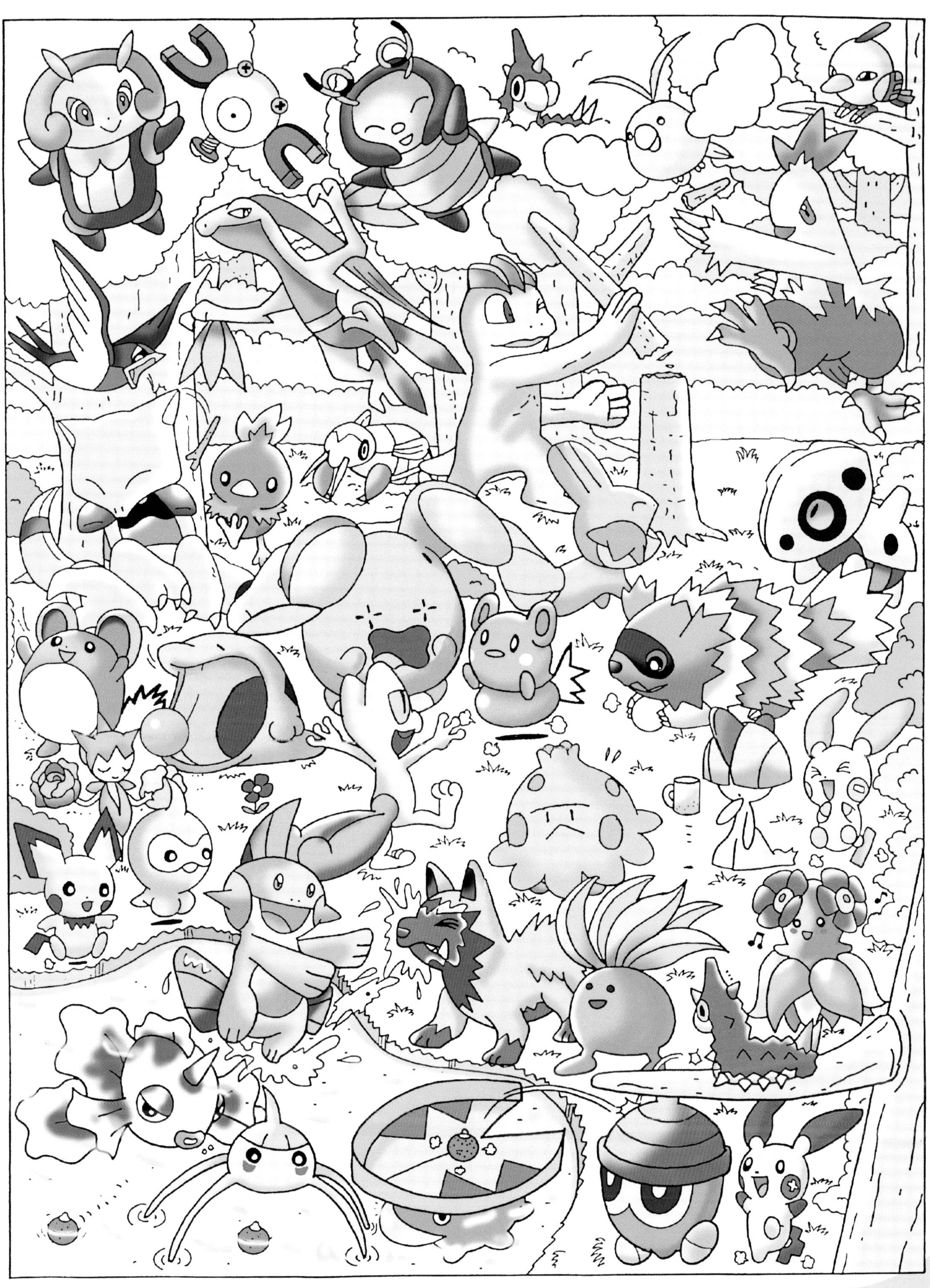

Hello Everyone: BIG MAZE

Pikachu and friends are going to see Latios, who is waiting at the FINISH. Make sure you greet each Pokémon you meet on your way to the FINISH.

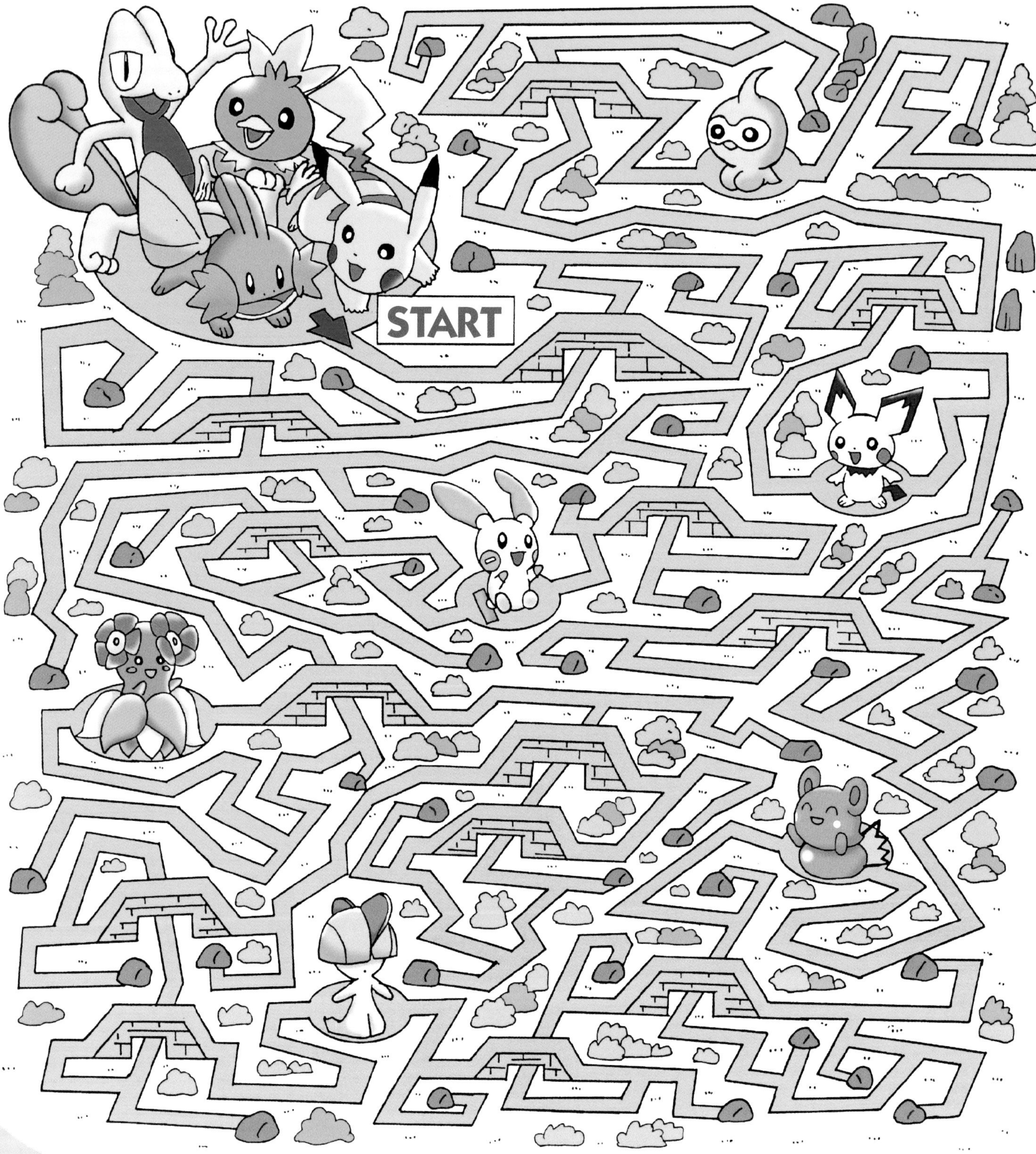
START

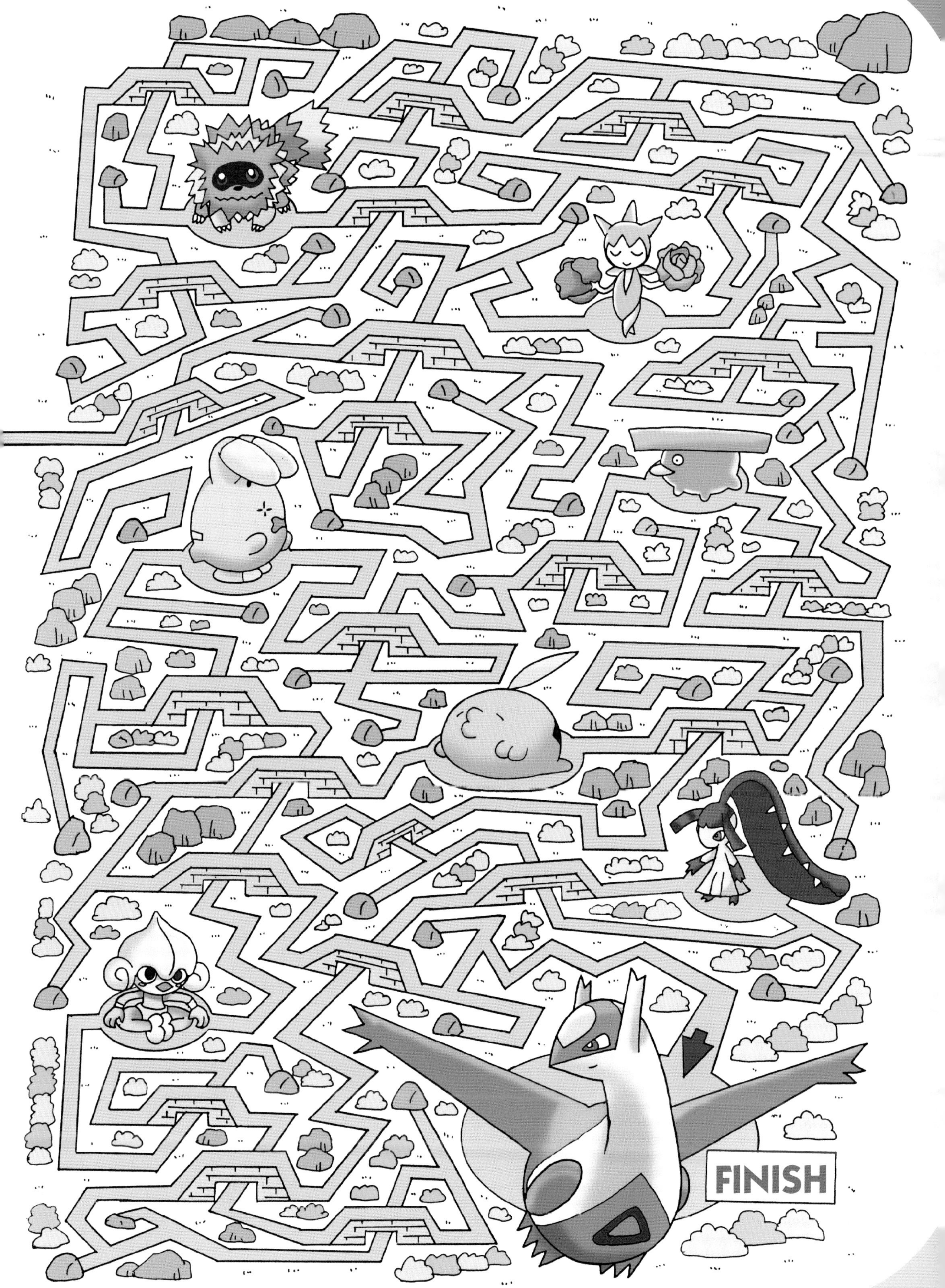
FINISH

Zoom-in Puzzle

See the flying Pokémon below? Can you match the close-ups in circles A, B, C and D with the flying Pokémon?

A
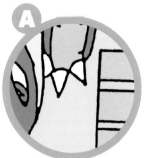

B
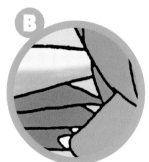

C
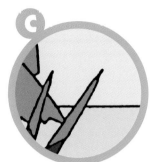

D

"Who Switched?" Puzzle

Look at the Pokémon in the panels below. Which pairs of Pokémon have switched their positions? Hint: Two pairs of Pokémon did this.

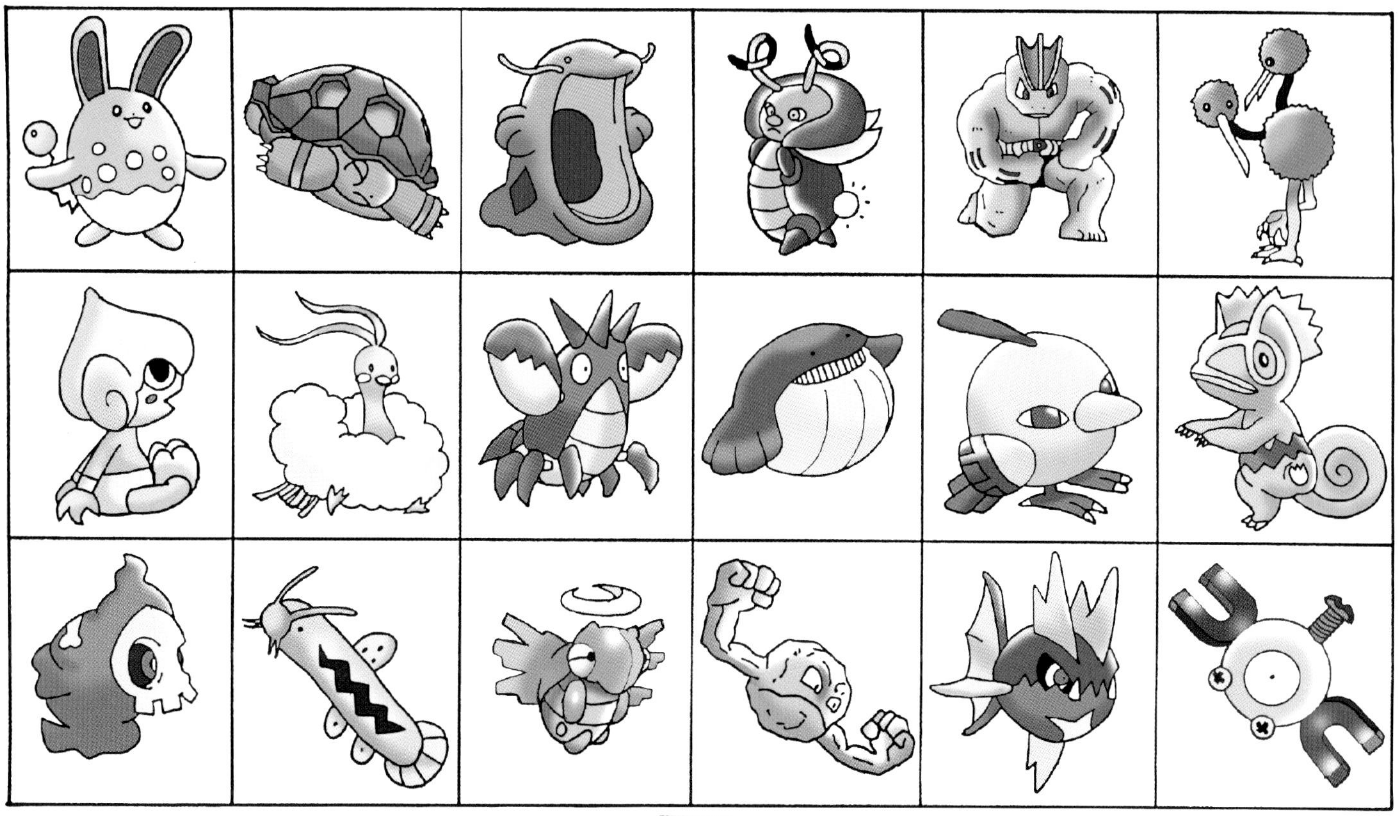

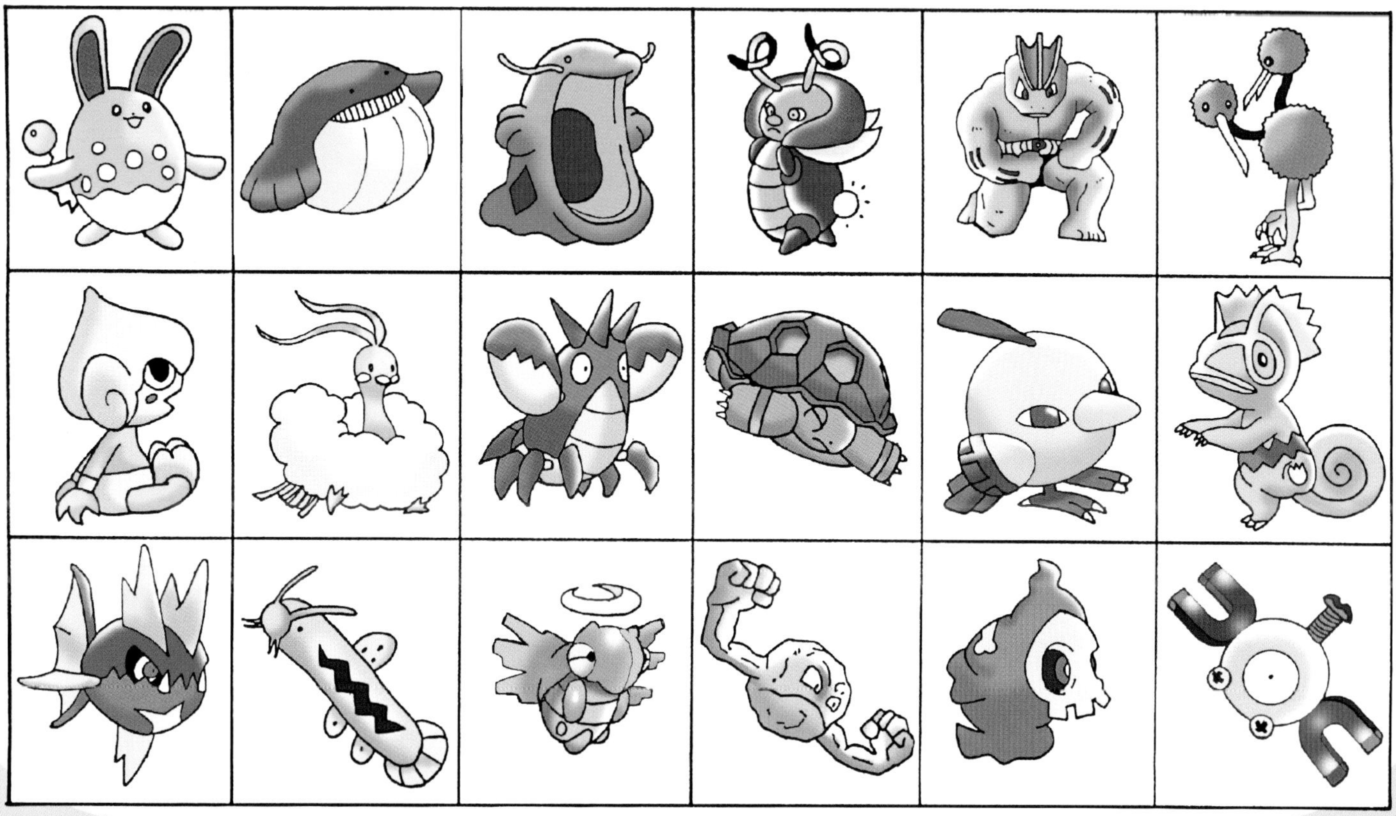

Pipe Maze

🔴 **Find out which Pokémon meets a Pokémon of the same type.**

Pipe Maze Rule:

Start from the top and go down. Every time you come to a corner, you must turn.

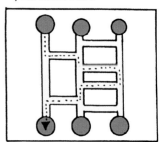

Electric-type	Water-type	Fire-type	Fighting-type	Psychic-type

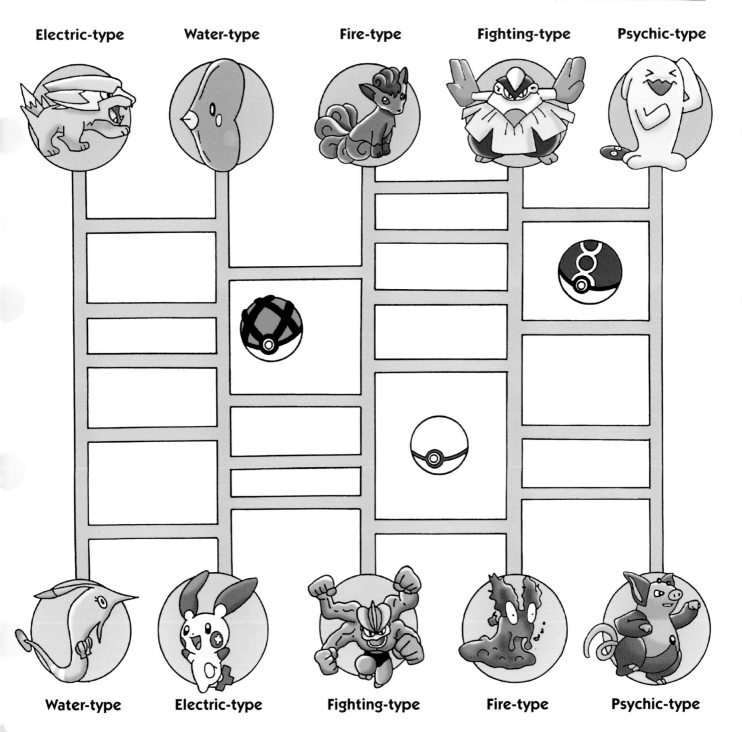

Water-type	Electric-type	Fighting-type	Fire-type	Psychic-type

8

"Find the Same Groups" Puzzle

Can you tell which rows below contain the same Pokémon? Answer by giving the numbers of the rows.

1

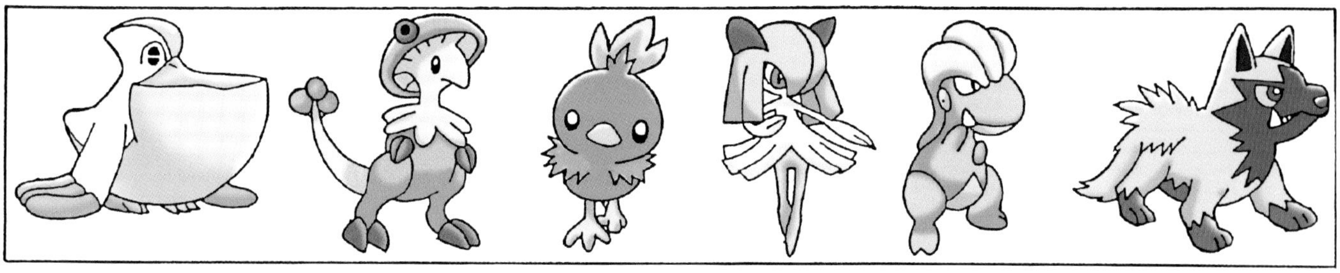

2

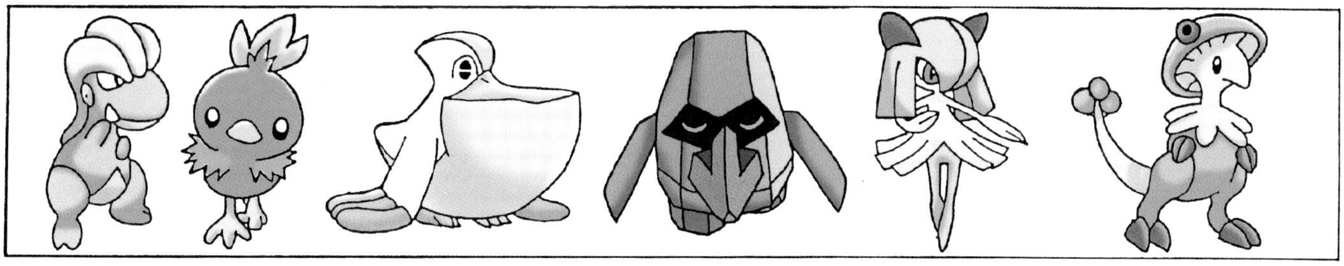

3

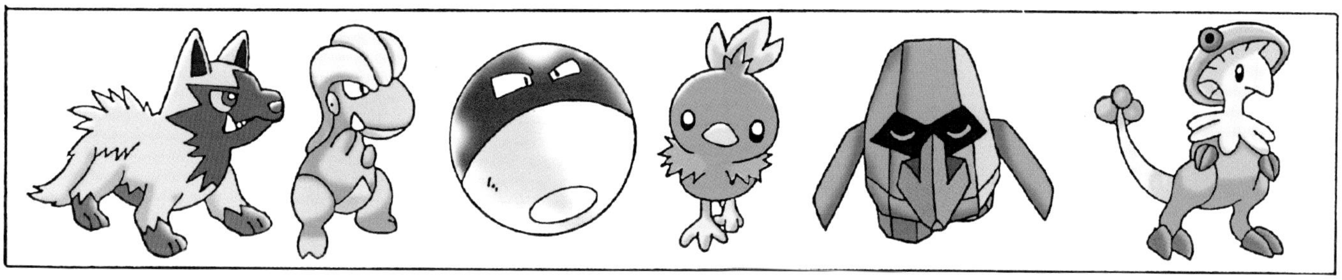

4

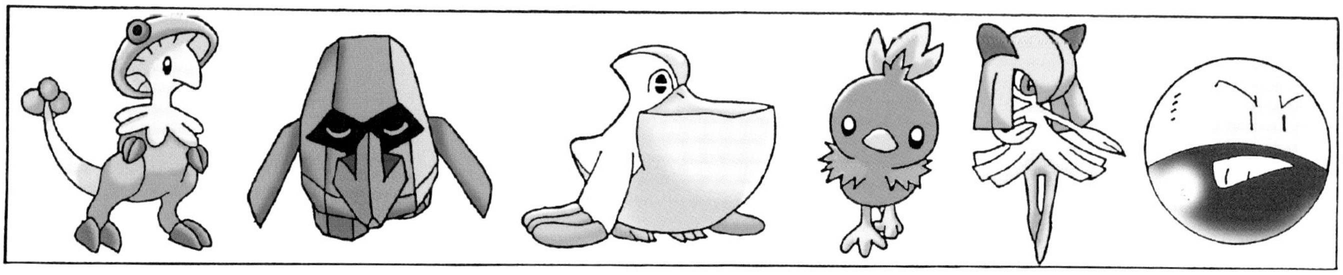

5

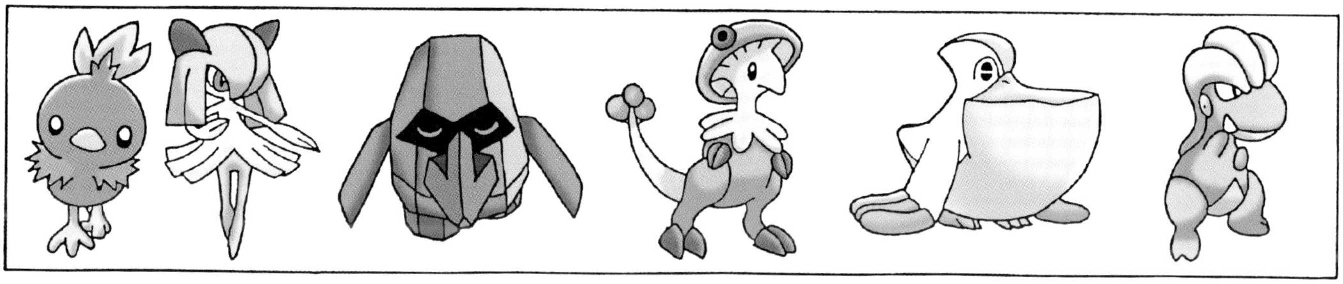

6

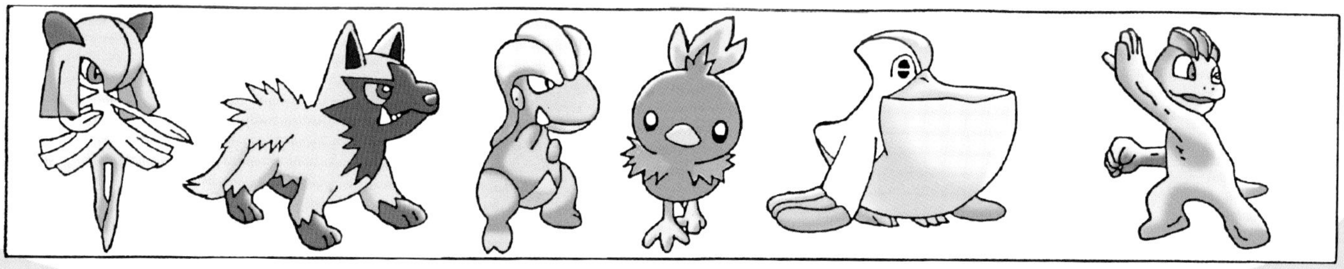

Friends Maze

Work your way to FINISH by passing through only water-type Pokémon.

START

★ Some water-type Pokémon are dead ends.

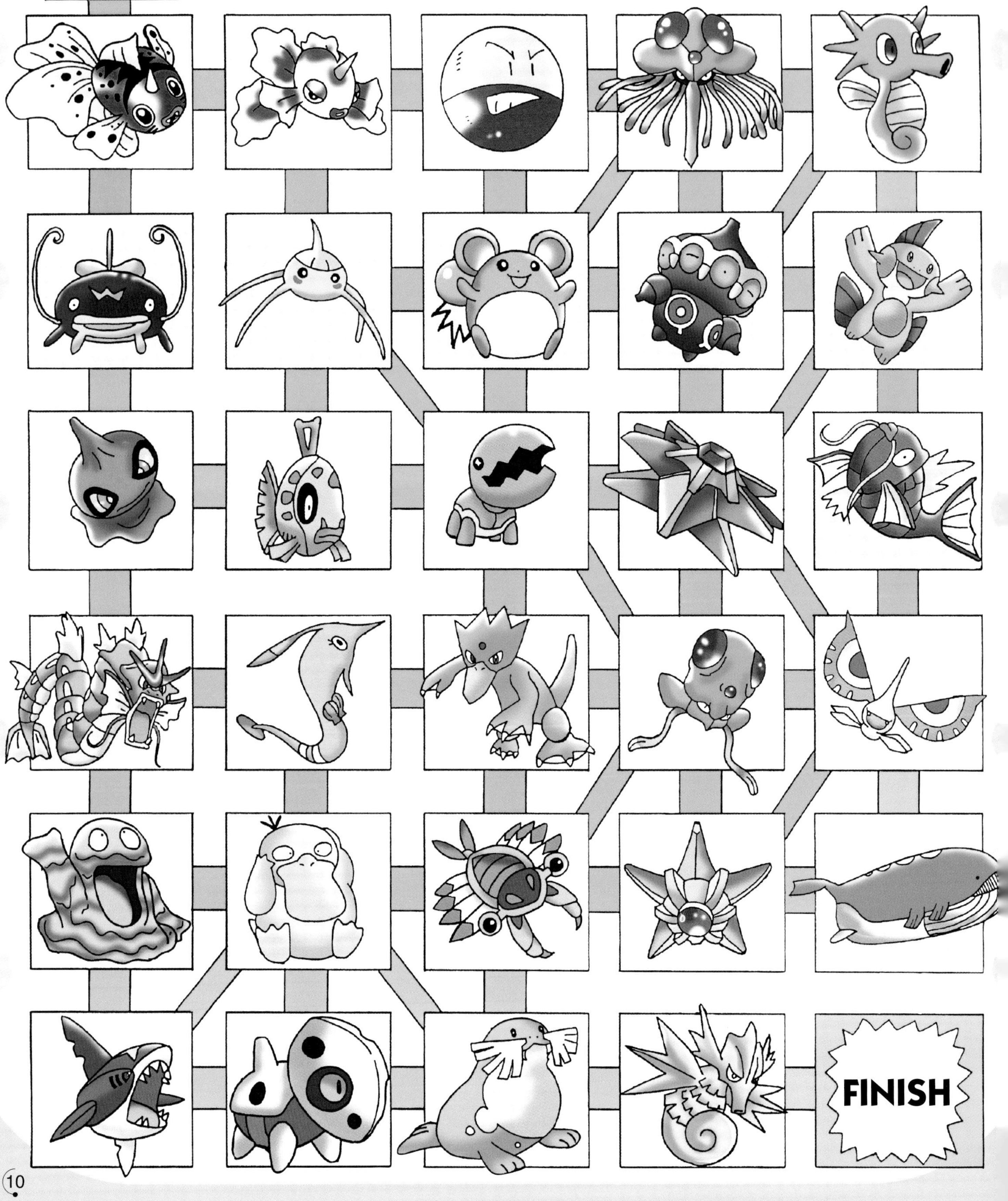
FINISH

Match-the-Disks Puzzle

Pictures are missing in the disks A through E. Select the pictures from the circles 1 through 10 shown below that belong in the disks A through E.

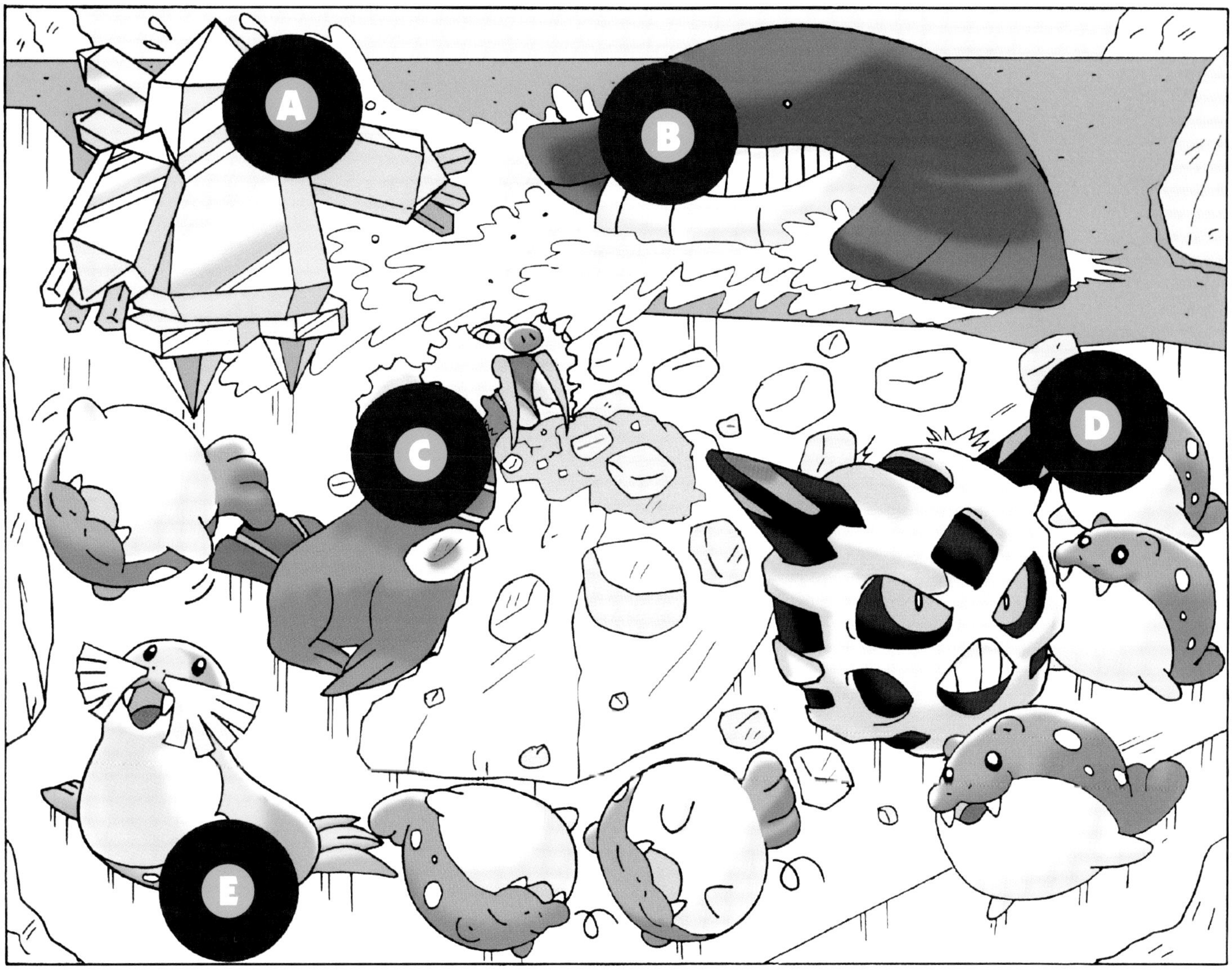
A
B
C
D
E

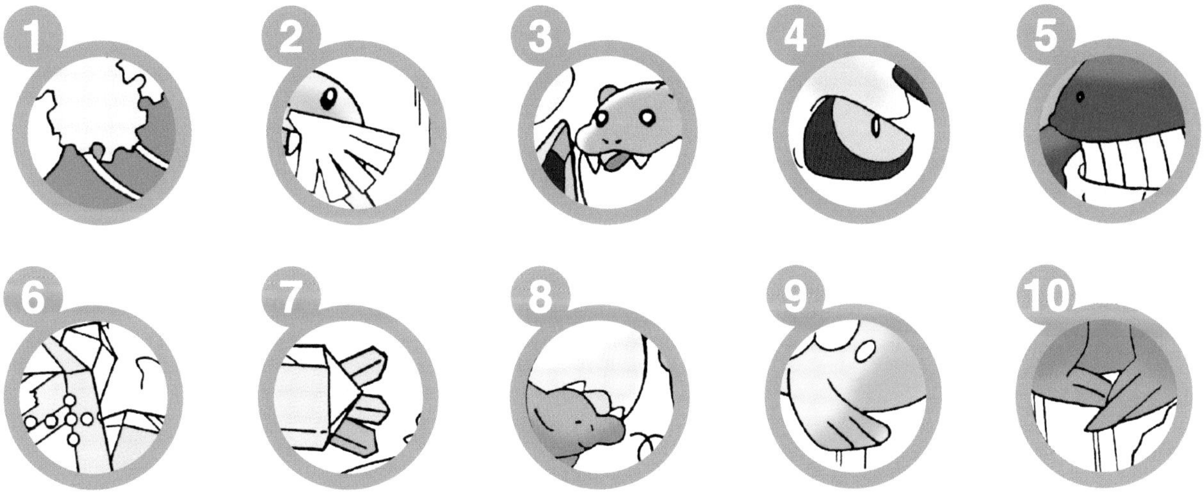
1
2
3
4
5
6
7
8
9
10

What Is Wrong With This Picture? 2

Pokémon are training hard in the rocky mountain!

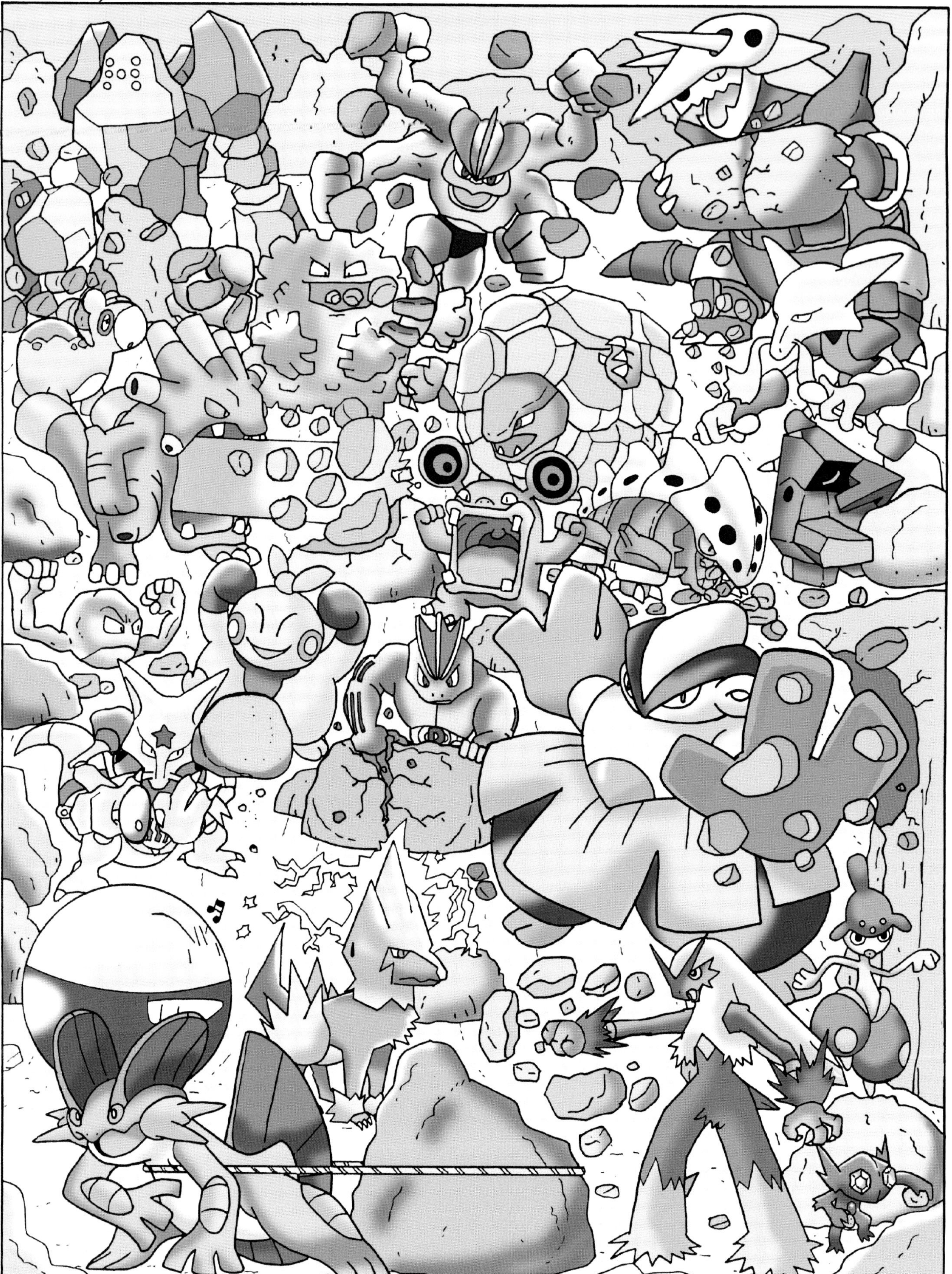

Can you find the 10 items that are different from the picture on the left?

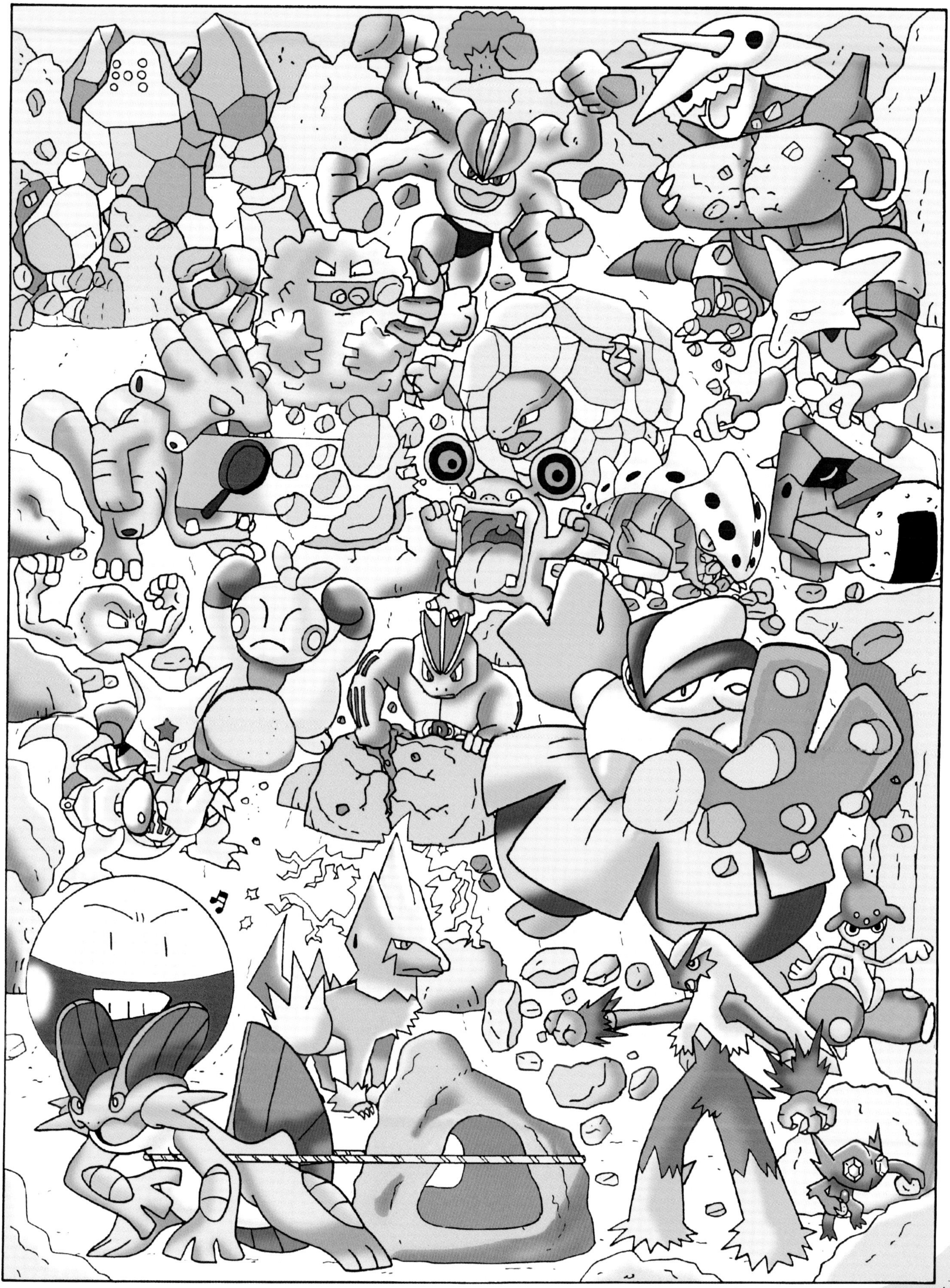

Evolution Maze

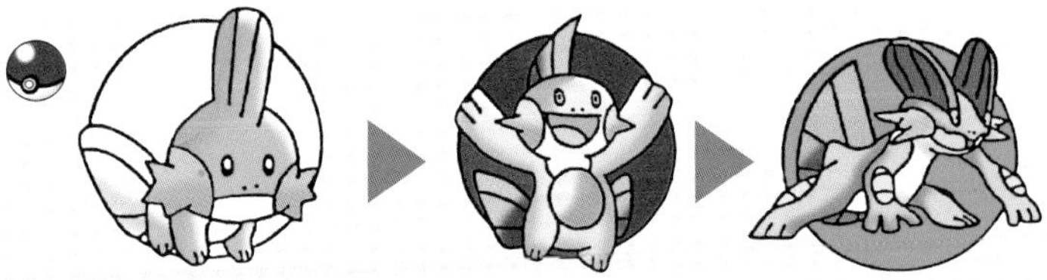

Move forward to FINISH, always passing from Mudkip to Marshtomp to Swampert.

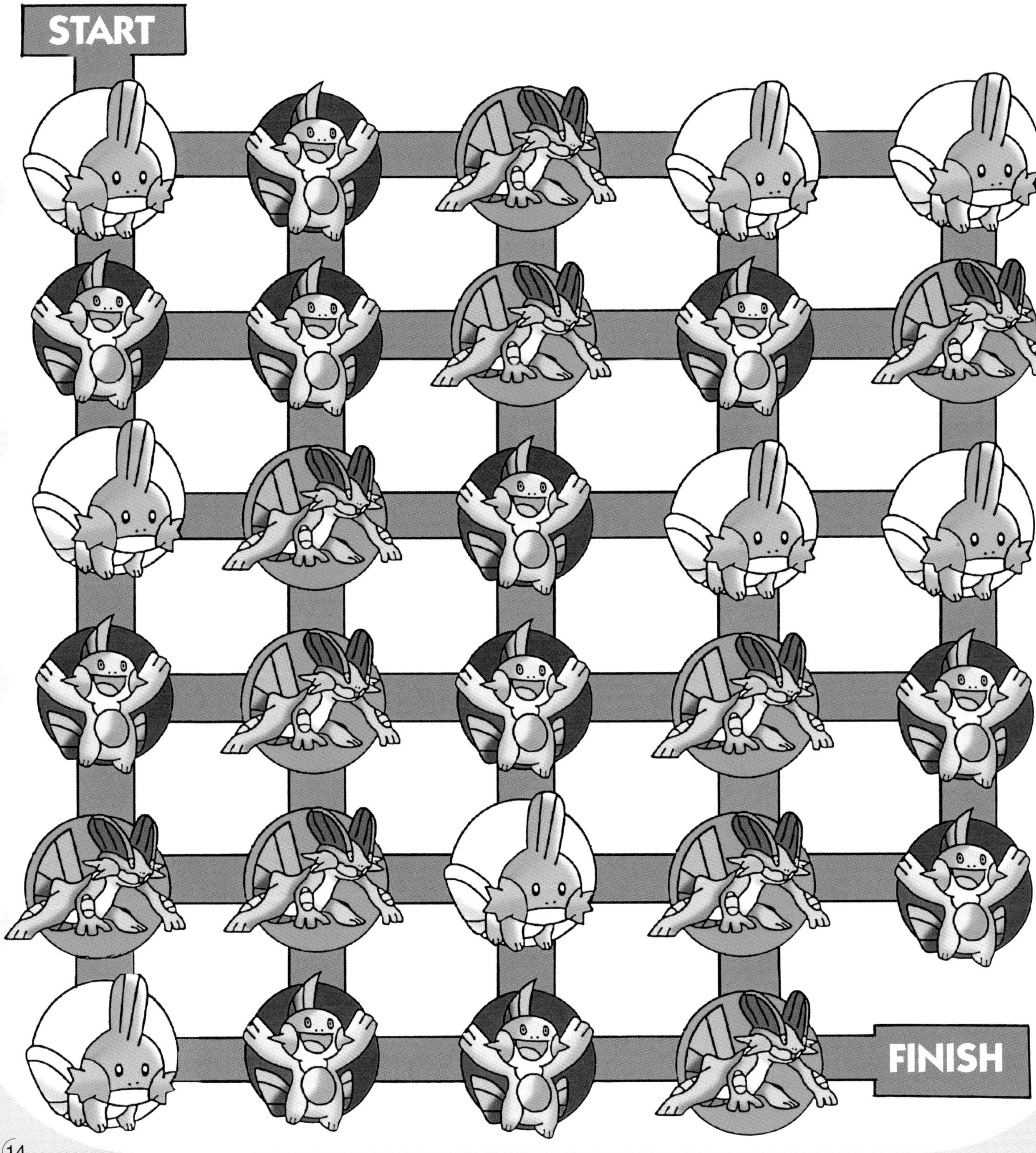
START
FINISH

Find Wrong Evolutions

Many Pokémon are shown evolving in three stages below. Two sets of Pokémon, however, are not evolving correctly. Find these sets.

1
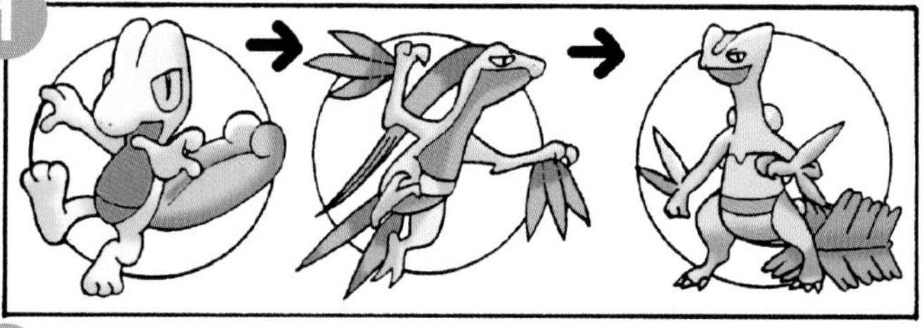

2
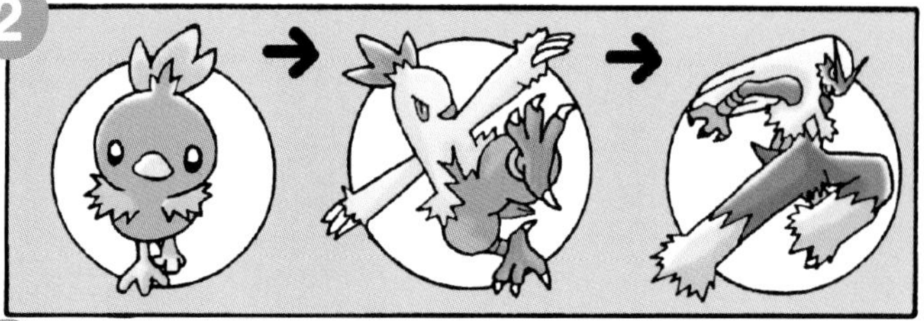

3
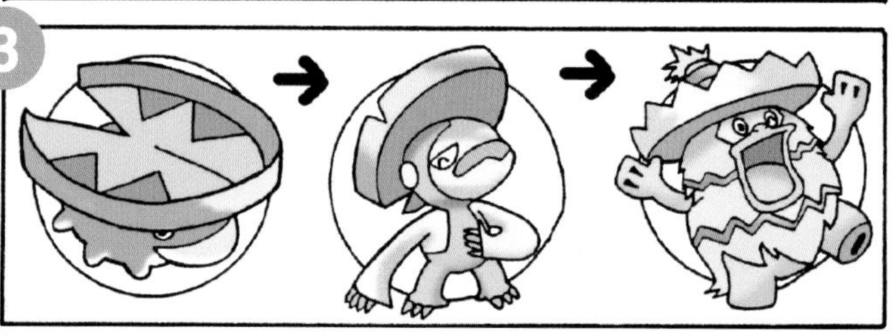

4
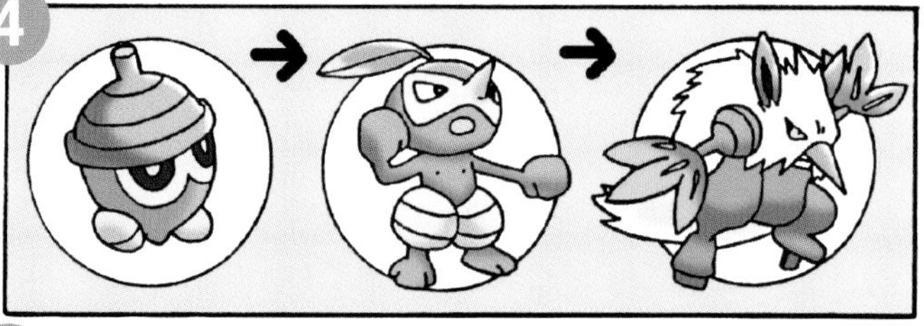

5
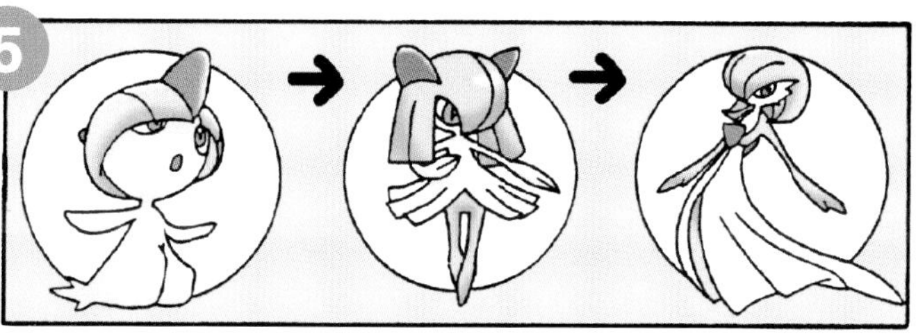

6
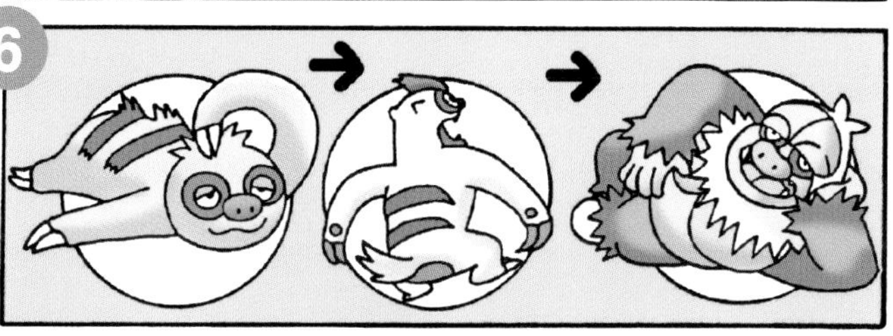

7
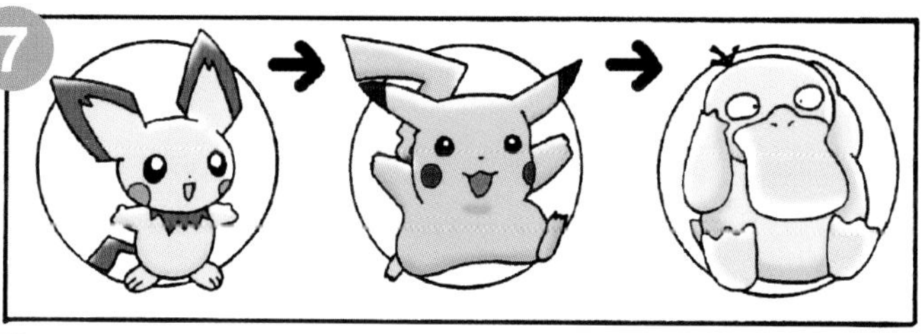

8
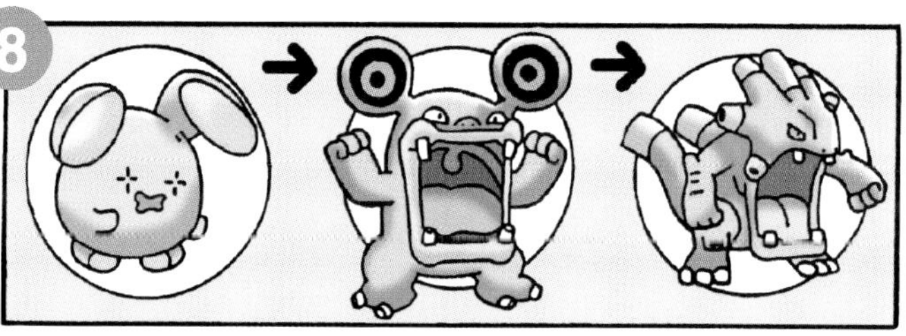

9
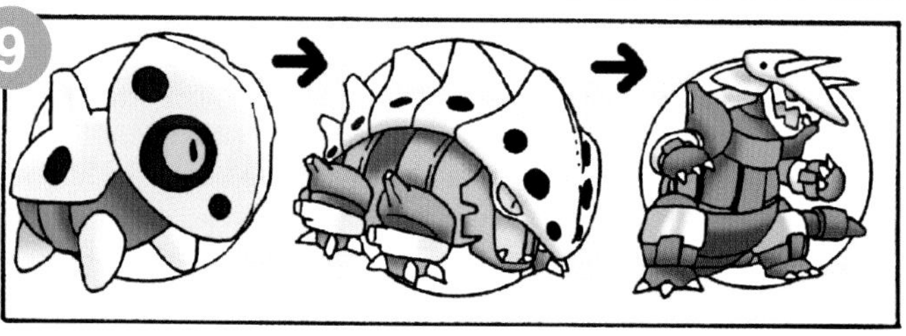

10
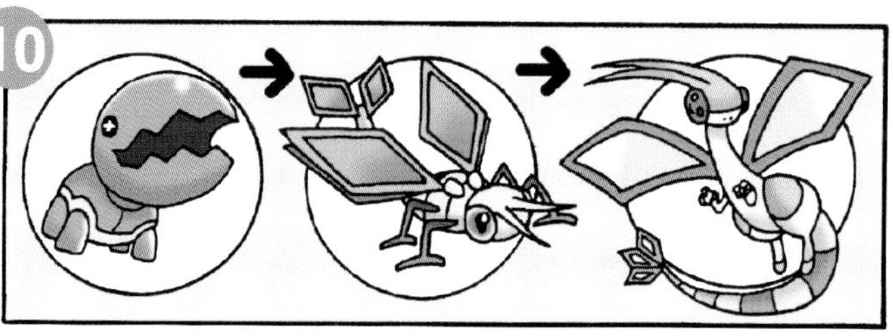

11
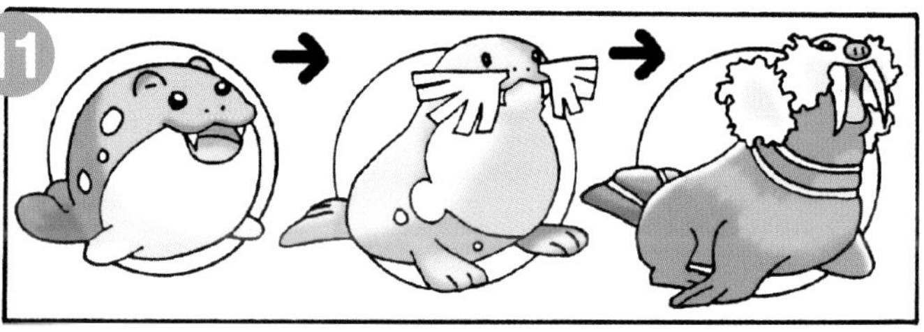

12
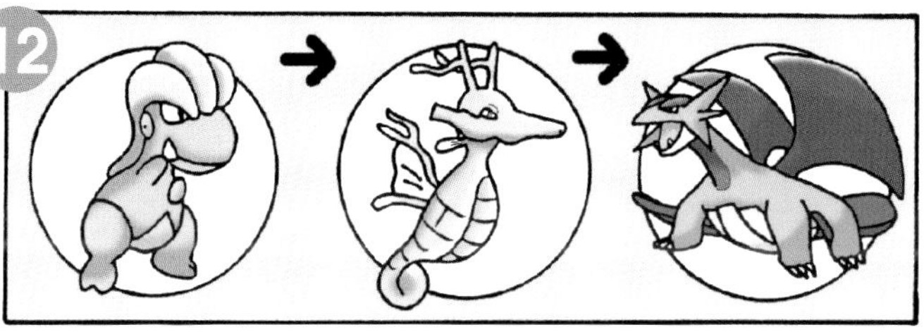

13
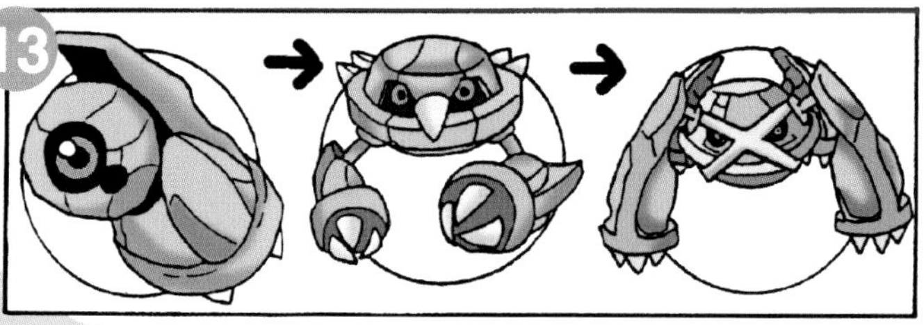

14
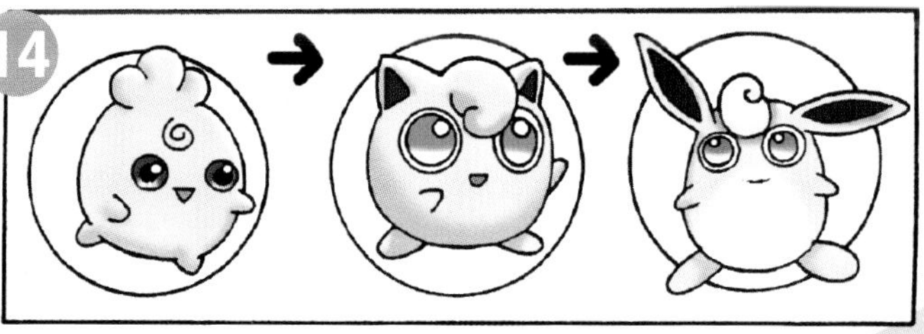

Silhouette Puzzle

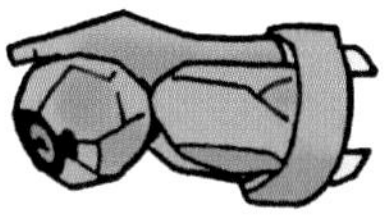

Pokémon are in the desert. Can you tell which silhouettes on the left fit into the picture from A through E?

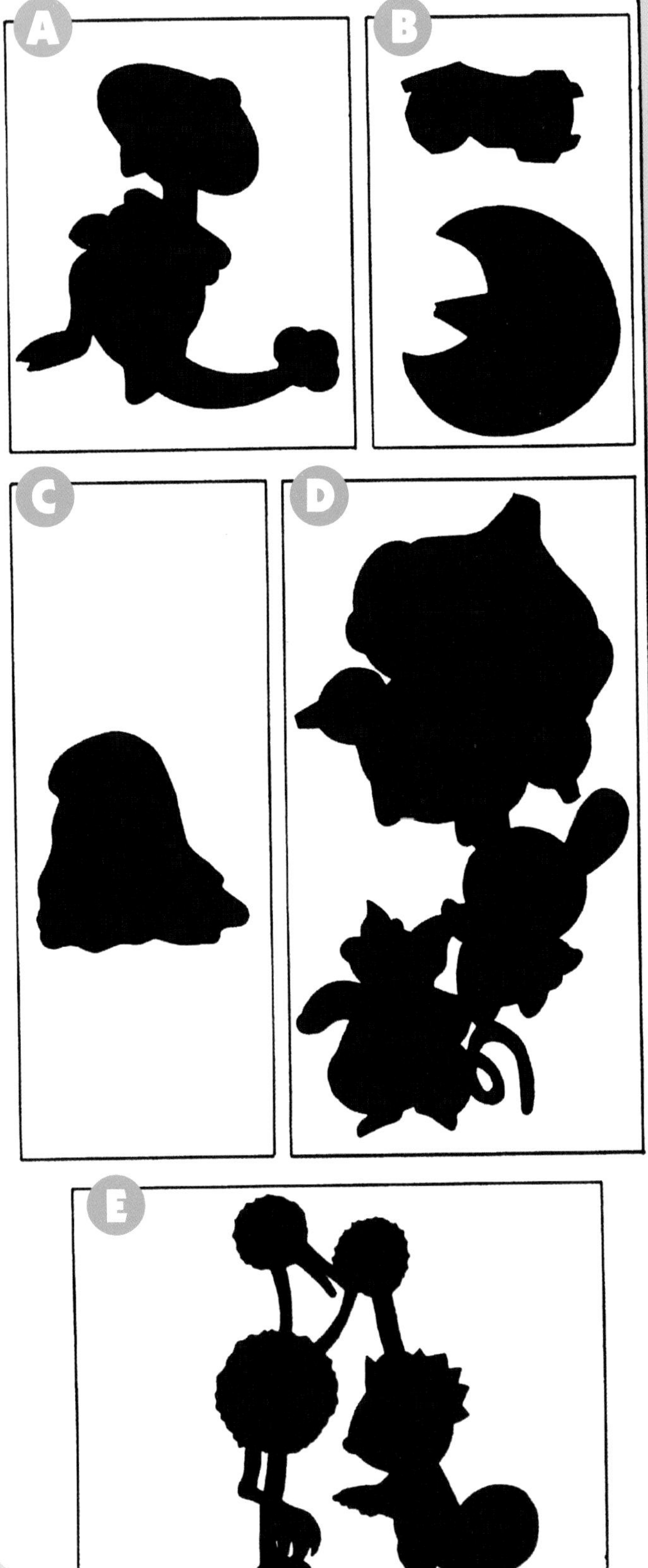
A
B
C
D
E

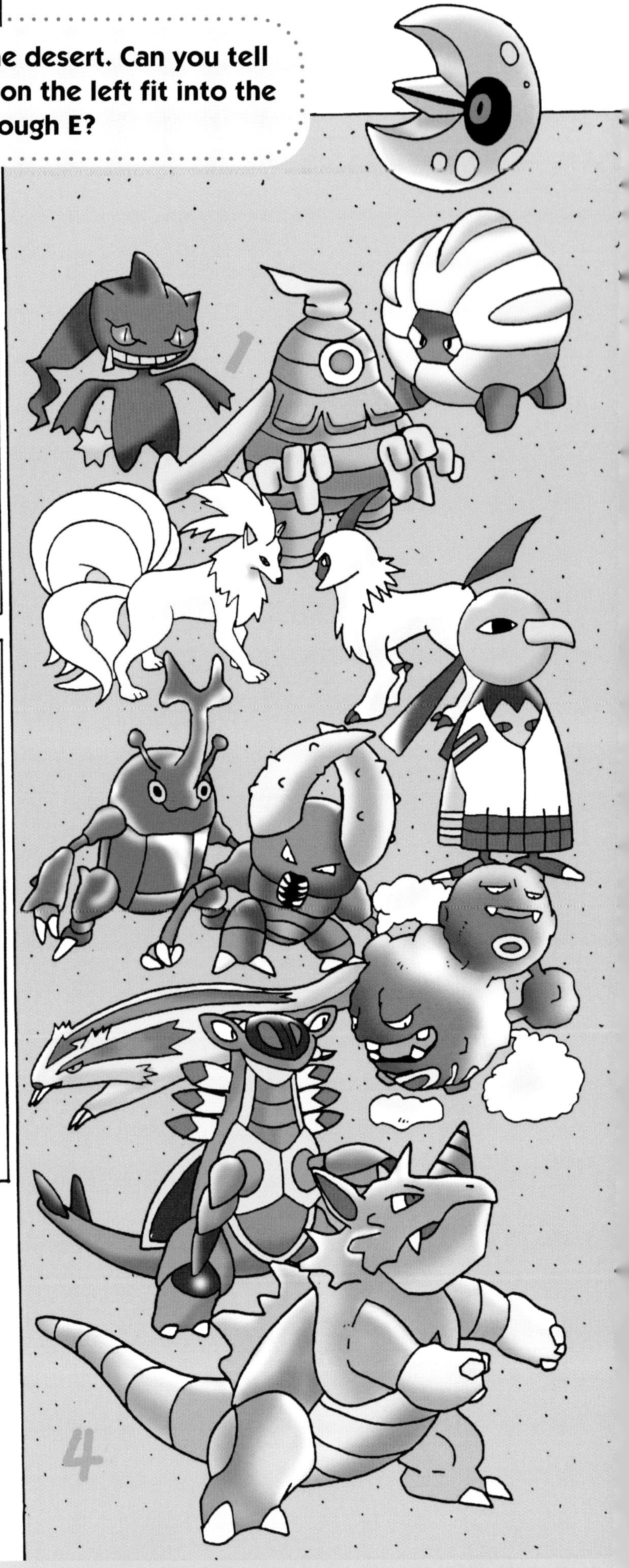
1
4

★ **Numbers 1 through 9 are hidden in the desert. Let's find them!**

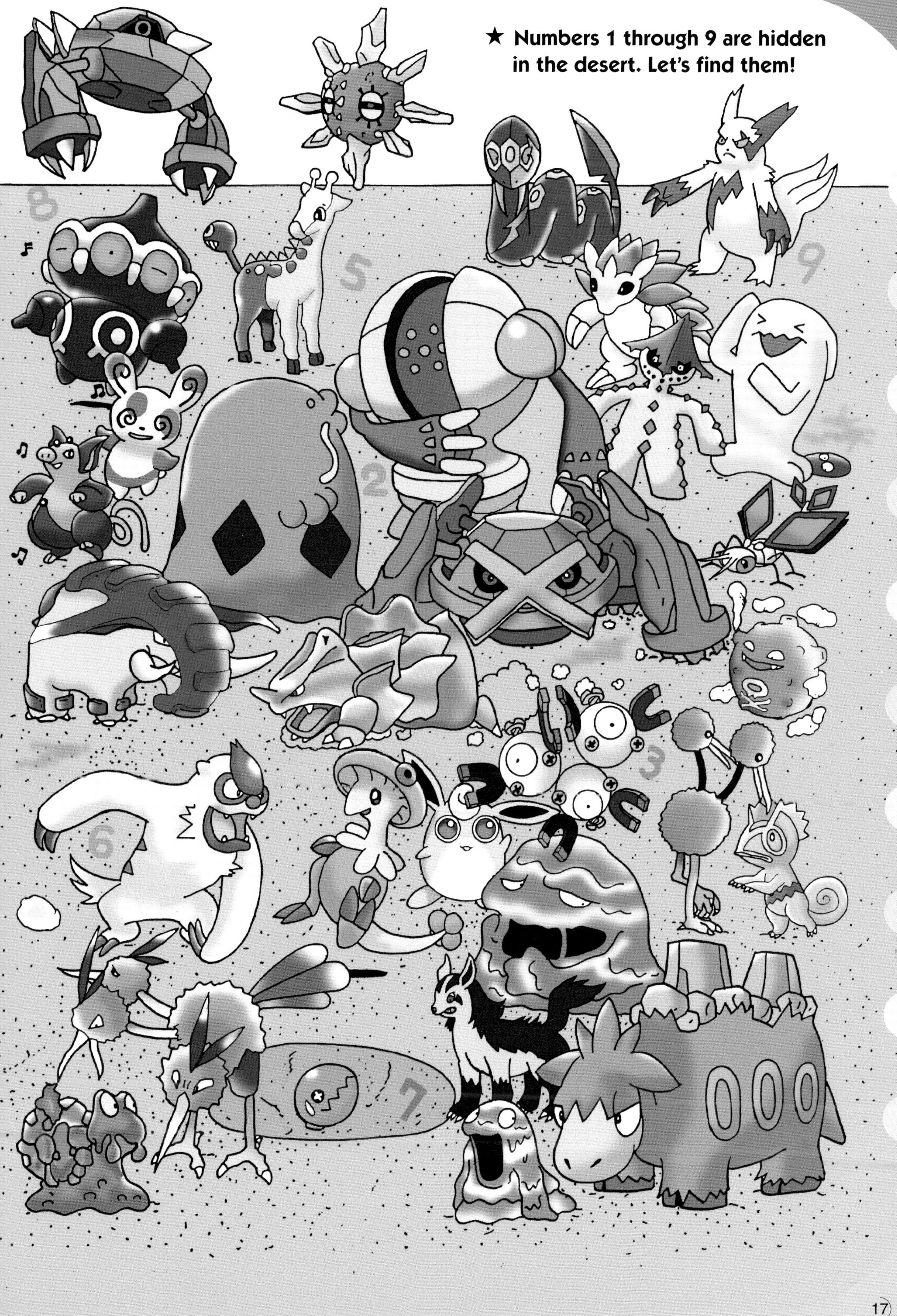

Eyes Maze

We don't know which hideout Treecko and his friends are heading for. Is it 1, 2 or 3? Let's find out by following the direction of the Pokémon's gazes.

★ The eyes in the maze below belong to six different Pokémon. Can you tell who these six Pokémon are?

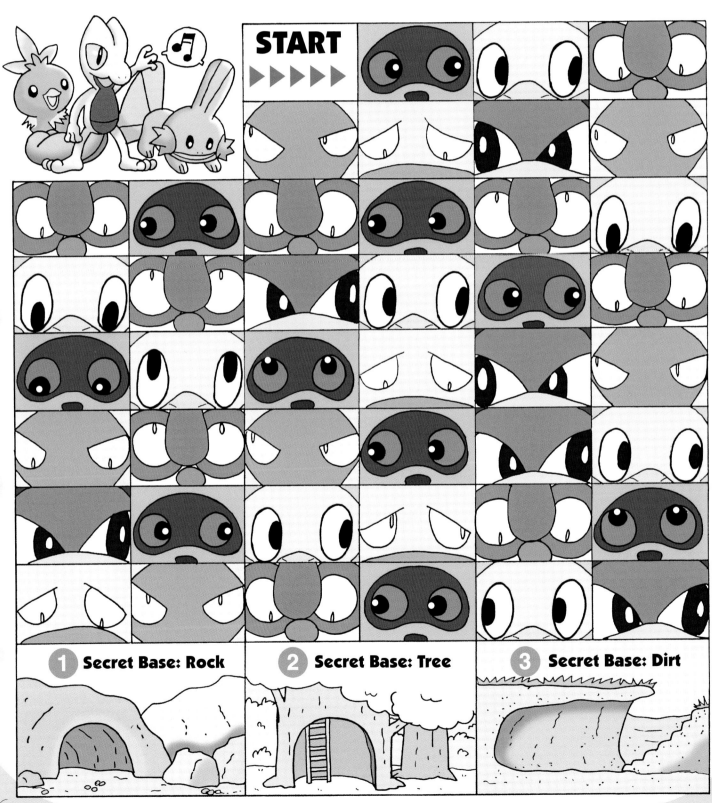

START
▶▶▶▶▶

1 Secret Base: Rock

2 Secret Base: Tree

3 Secret Base: Dirt

Hide-and-Seek

Pokémon are playing hide-and-seek. Ludicolo is the seeker. The five Pokémon listed below are hiding somewhere in the picture. Let's find them! You can see only part of them, so you'll have to search very carefully.

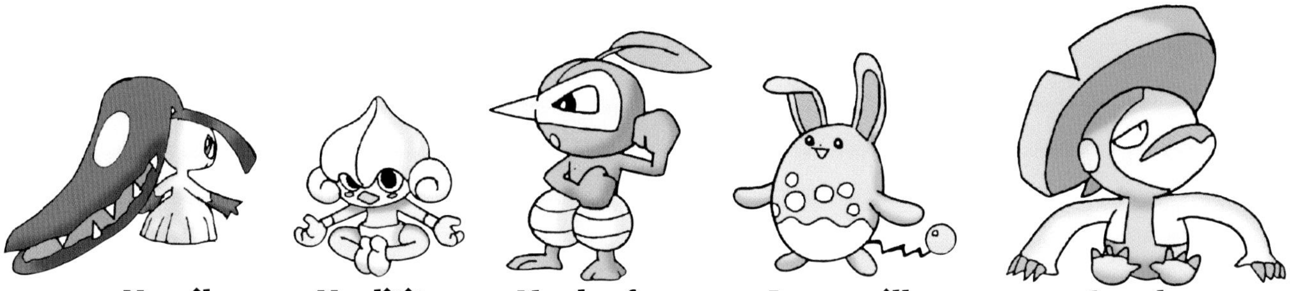

Mawile **Meditite** **Nuzleaf** **Azumarill** **Lombre**

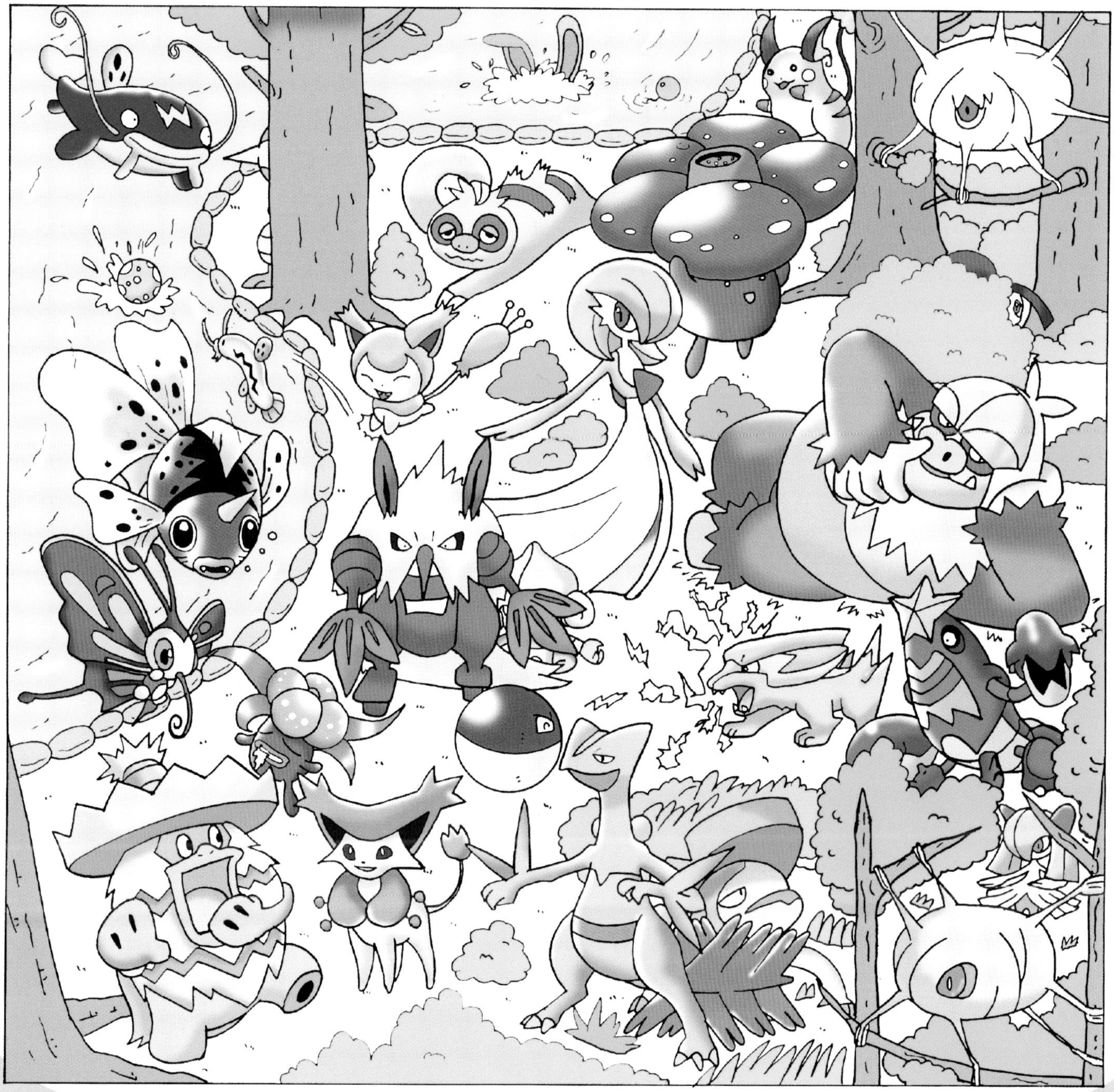

Select and Go!

Choose the right answer and proceed to FINISH.

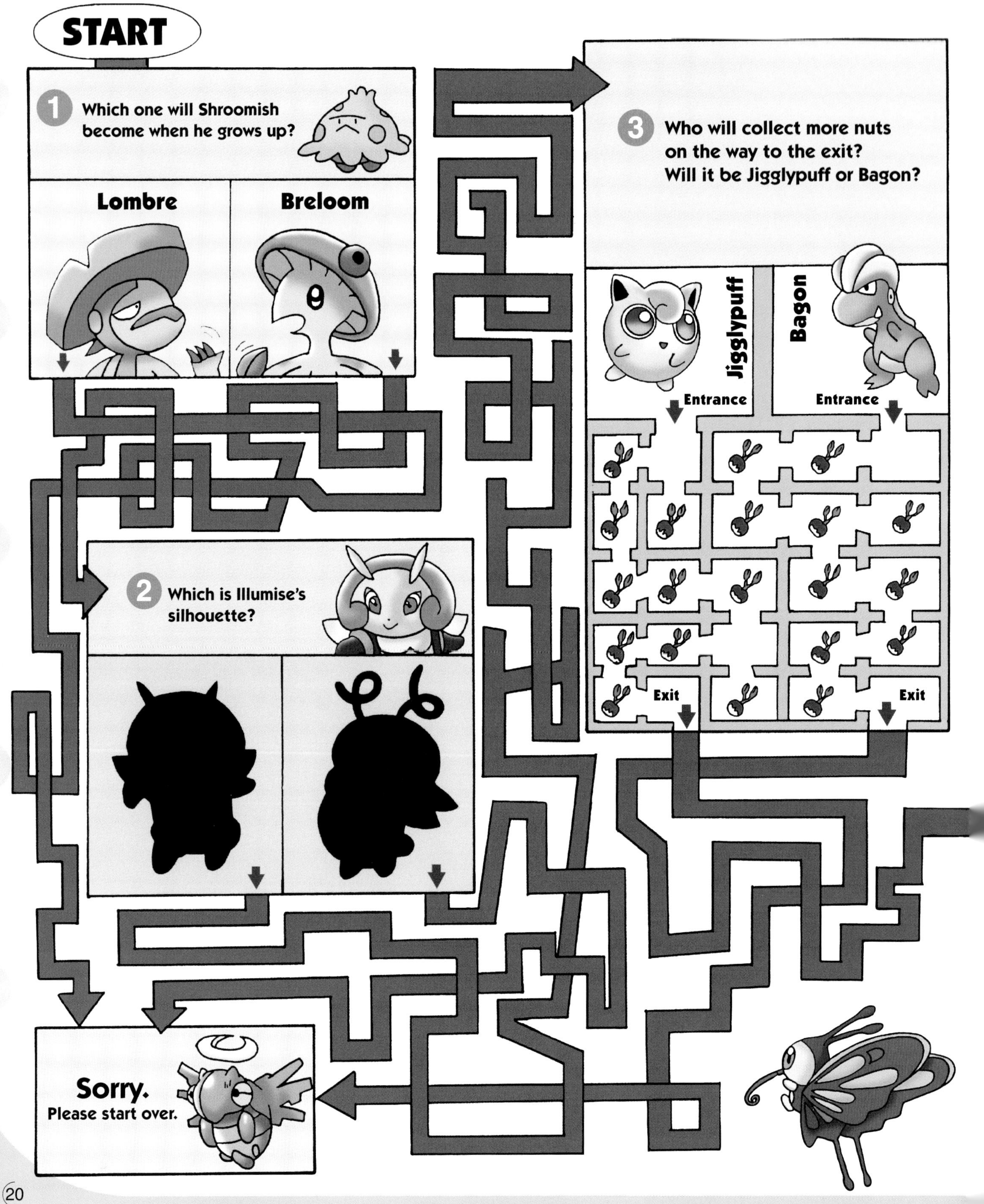

START
1 Which one will Shroomish become when he grows up?
Lombre
Breloom
2 Which is Illumise's silhouette?
3 Who will collect more nuts on the way to the exit? Will it be Jigglypuff or Bagon?
Jigglypuff
Bagon
Entrance
Entrance
Exit
Exit
Sorry.
Please start over.

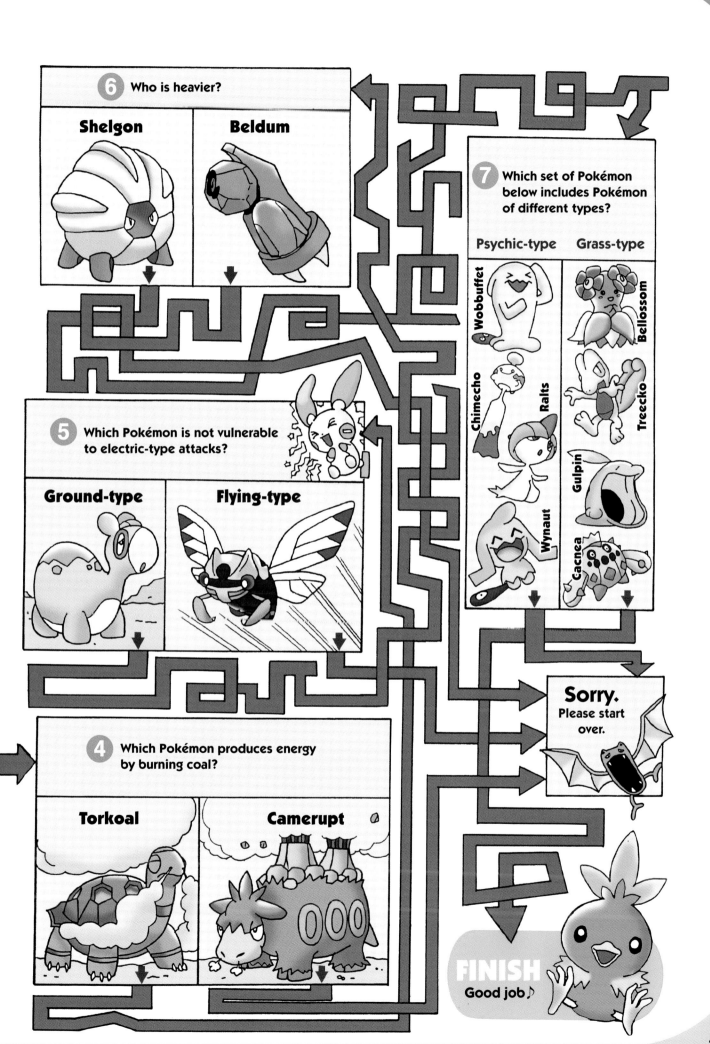

6 Who is heavier?

Shelgon

Beldum

7 Which set of Pokémon below includes Pokémon of different types?

Psychic-type   Grass-type

Wobbuffet

Bellossom

Chimecho   Ralts   Treecko

Gulpin

Wynaut   Cacnea

5 Which Pokémon is not vulnerable to electric-type attacks?

Ground-type

Flying-type

Sorry.
Please start over.

4 Which Pokémon produces energy by burning coal?

Torkoal

Camerupt

FINISH
Good job ♪

What Is Wrong With This Picture? 3

It looks like they're having a good time underwater.

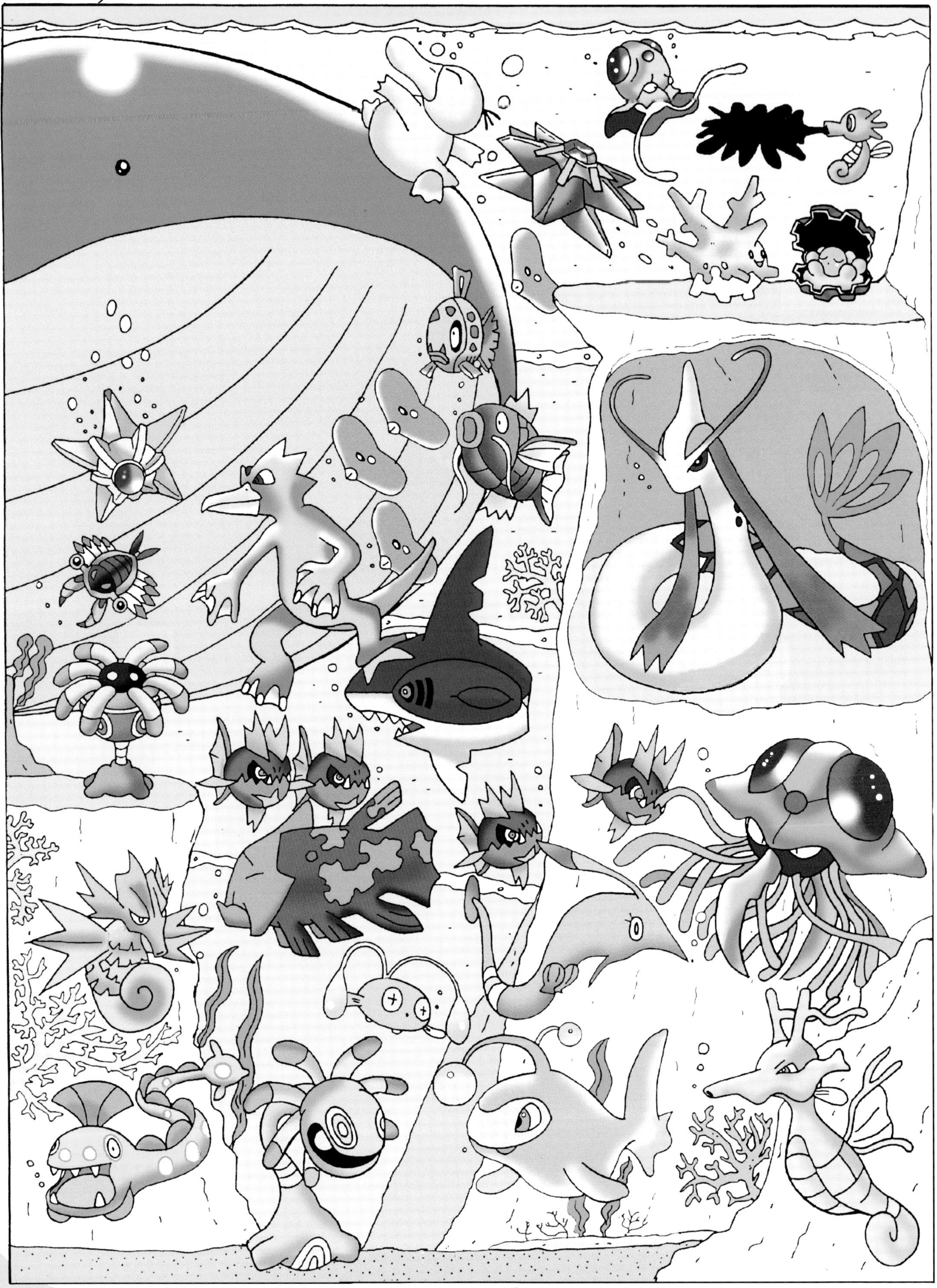

Circle each of the 10 items that are different in the picture on the left.

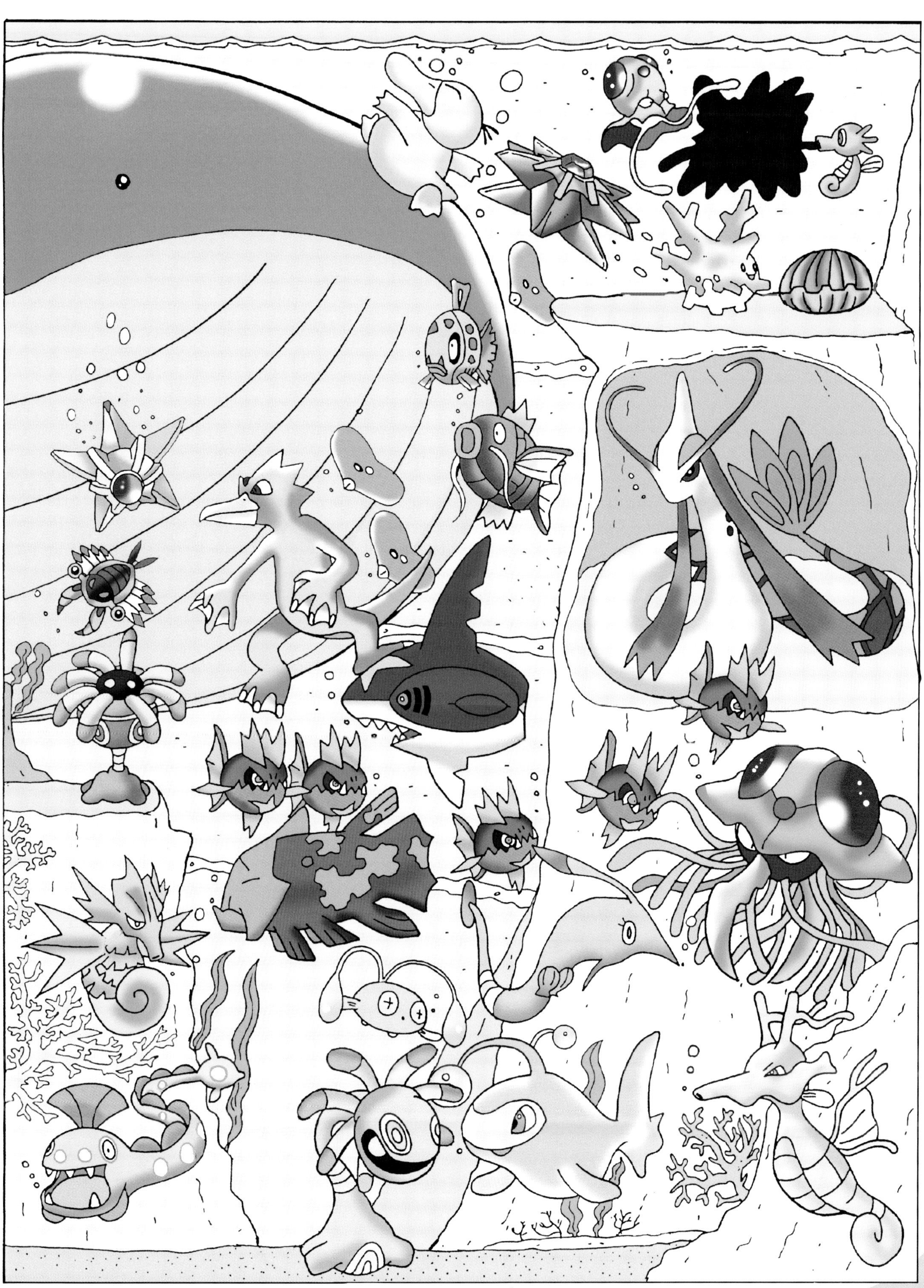

Pokémon-Shape Maze

Work your way through to FINISH.

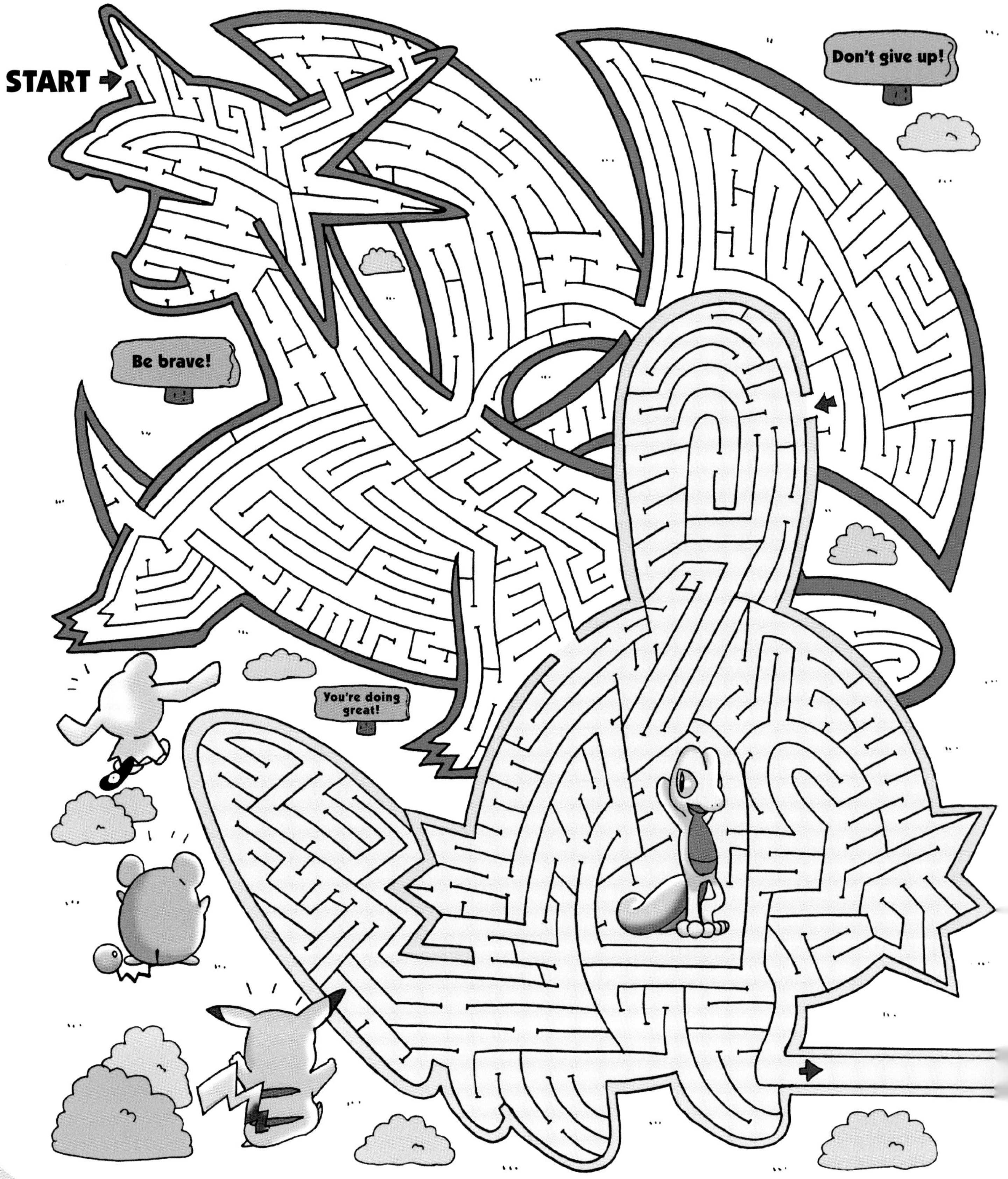

START
Don't give up!
Be brave!
You're doing great!

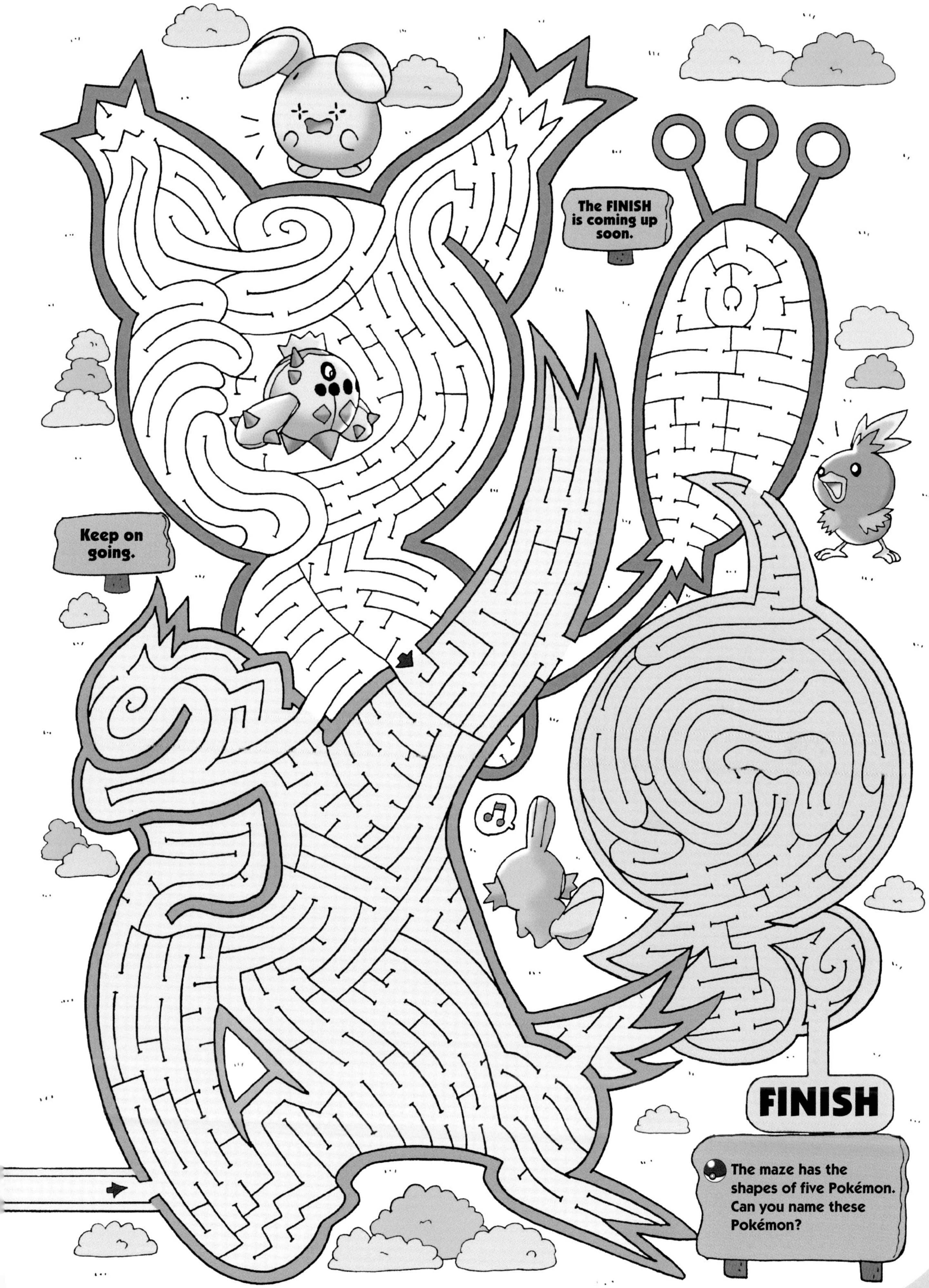

The FINISH is coming up soon.
Keep on going.
FINISH
The maze has the shapes of five Pokémon. Can you name these Pokémon?

Who Is Missing a Friend?

All but two of the Pokémon below have a twin. Can you name the two Pokémon who don't have friends?

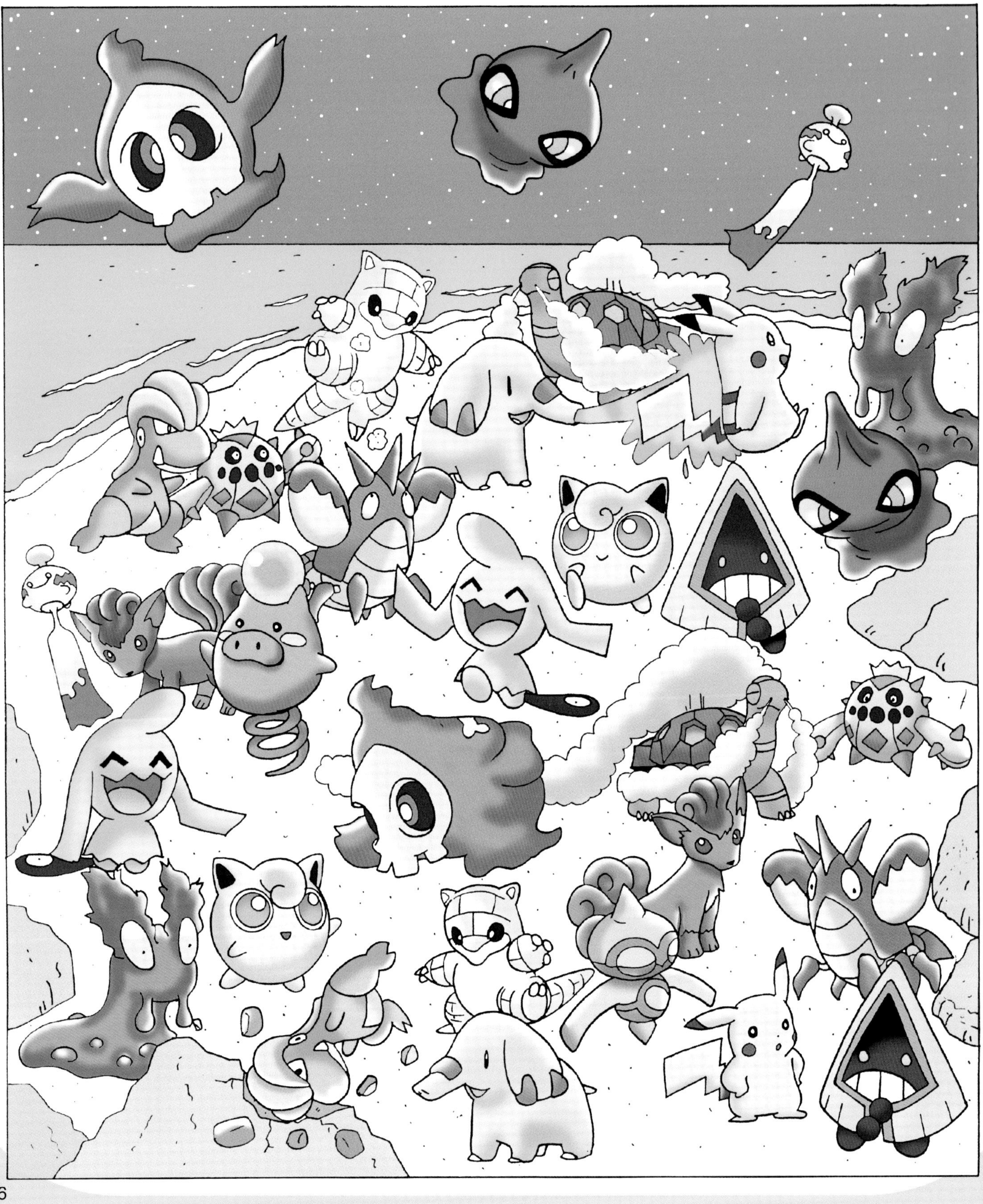

ANSWERS

Cover Maze

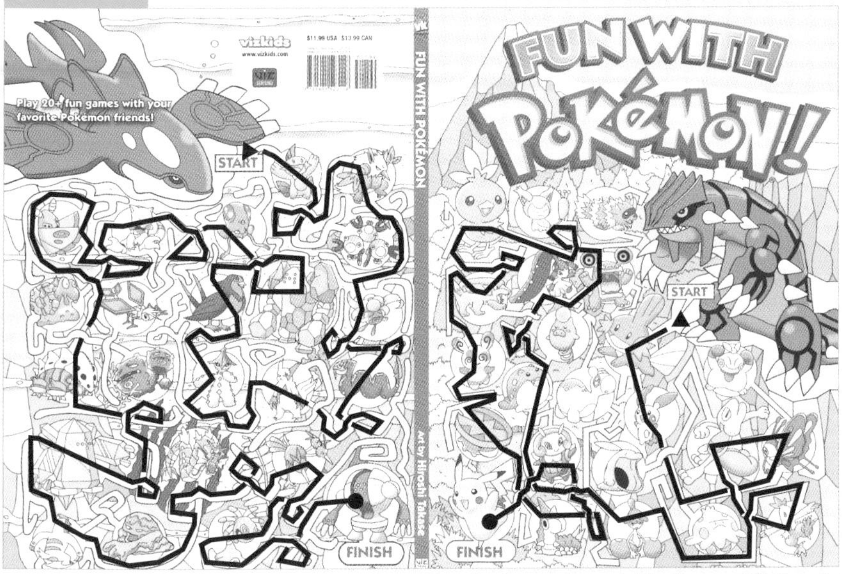
Play 20+ fun games with your favorite Pokémon friends!
FUN WITH POKéMON
FUN WITH POKéMON!
Art by Hiroshi Takase
START
START
FINISH
FINISH

You don't pass through Blaziken and Relicanth.

Which Pose Appears Twice? Page 1

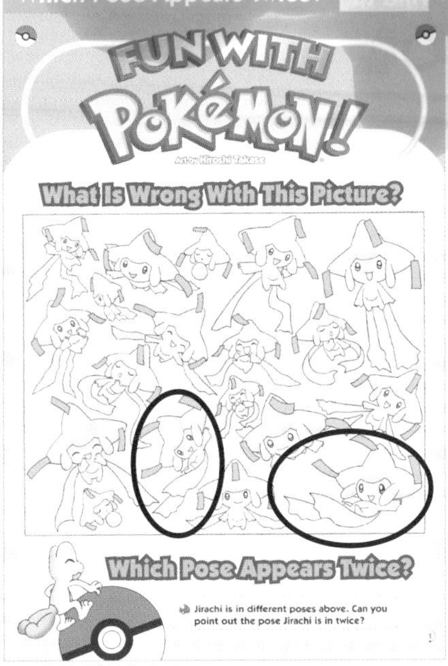
FUN WITH POKéMON!
Art by Hiroshi Takase
What Is Wrong With This Picture?
Which Pose Appears Twice?
Jirachi is in different poses above. Can you point out the pose Jirachi is in twice?

What Is Wrong With This Picture? Page 3

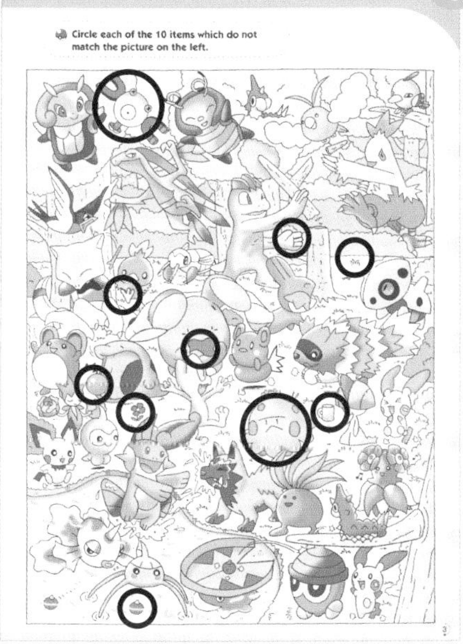
Circle each of the 10 items which do not match the picture on the left.

Hello Everyone: Big Maze Pages 4-5

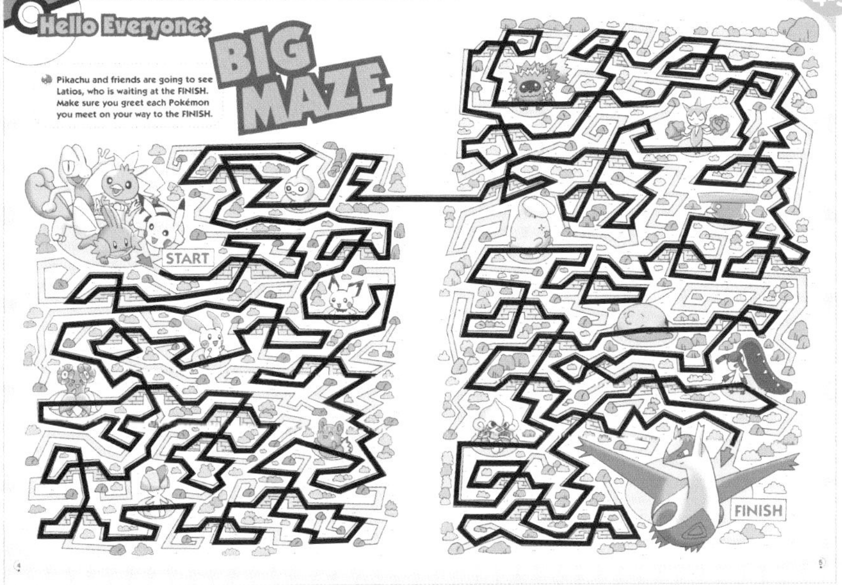
Hello Everyone: BIG MAZE
Pikachu and friends are going to see Latios, who is waiting at the FINISH. Make sure you greet each Pokémon you meet on your way to the FINISH.
START
FINISH

Zoom-In Puzzle Page 6

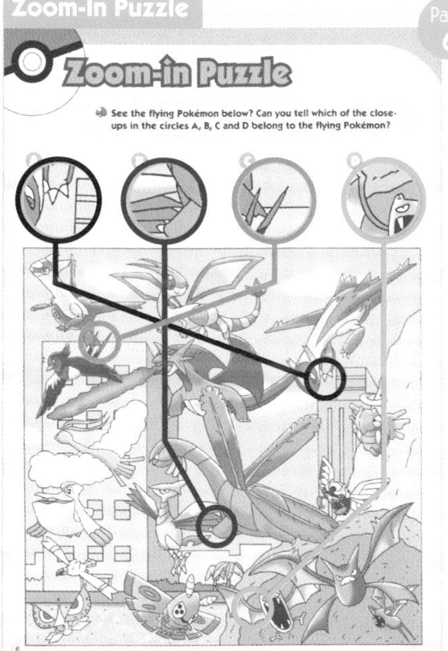
Zoom-in Puzzle
See the flying Pokémon below? Can you tell which of the close-ups in the circles A, B, C and D belong to the flying Pokémon?

"Who Switched?" Puzzle Page 7

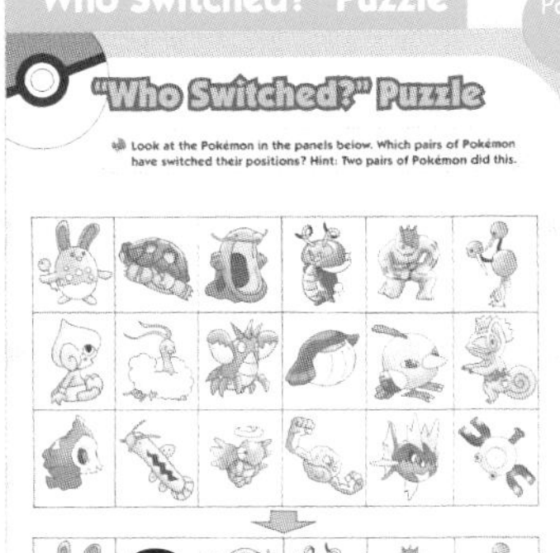
"Who Switched?" Puzzle
Look at the Pokémon in the panels below. Which pairs of Pokémon have switched their positions? Hint: Two pairs of Pokémon did this.

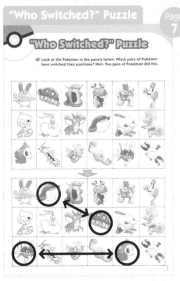

Torkoal in the top row and Wailmer in the middle row, and Duskull and Carvanha in the bottom row, have traded positions.

Pipe Maze Page 8

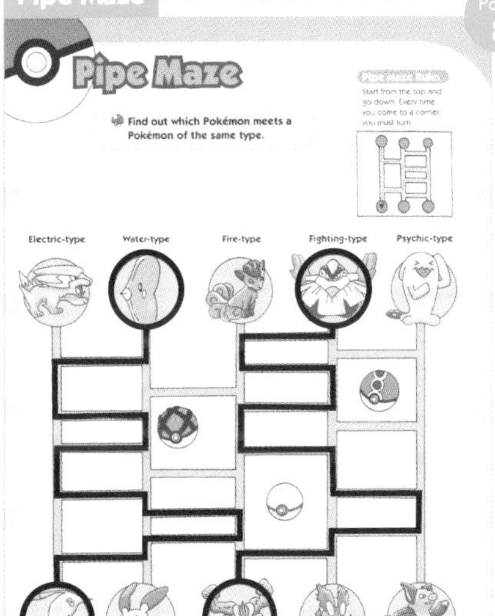
Pipe Maze
Find out which Pokémon meets a Pokémon of the same type.
Electric-type
Water-type
Fire-type
Fighting-type
Psychic-type
Water-type
Electric-type
Fighting-type
Fire-type
Psychic-type

ANSWERS

"Find the Same Groups" Puzzle

Page 9

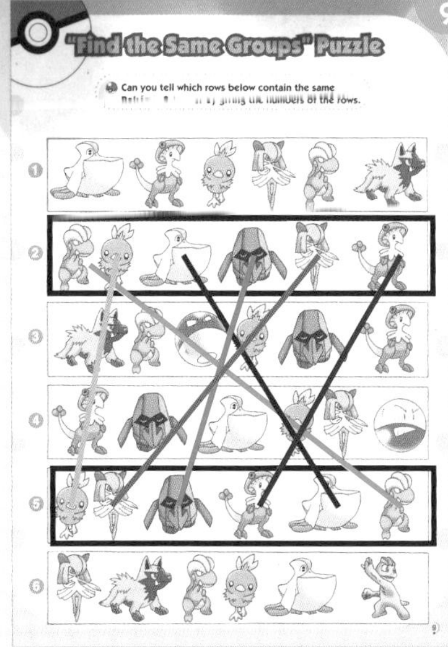

"Find the Same Groups" Puzzle

The answer is 2 and 5.

Friends Maze

Page 10

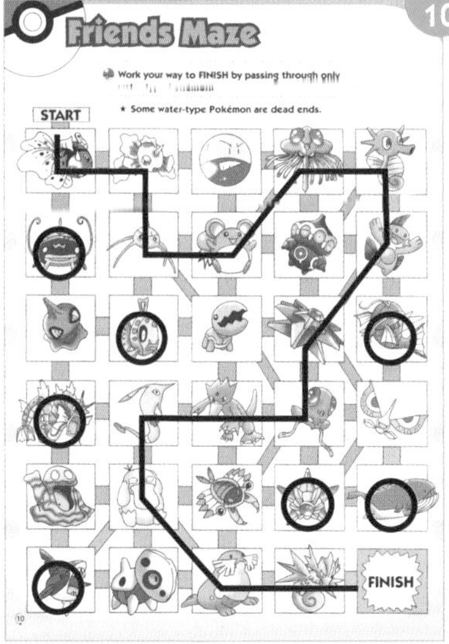

Friends Maze
Some water-type Pokémon are dead ends.
START
FINISH

You don't pass through the circled water-type Pokémon.

Match-the-Disk Puzzle

Page 11

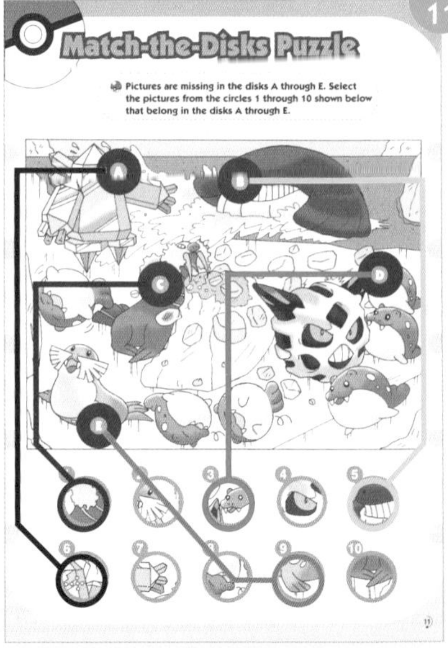

Match-the-Disks Puzzle
Pictures are missing in the disks A through E. Select the pictures from the circles 1 through 10 shown below that belong in the disks A through E.

A-6, B-5, C-1, D-3, E-9.

What Is Wrong With This Picture?

Page 13

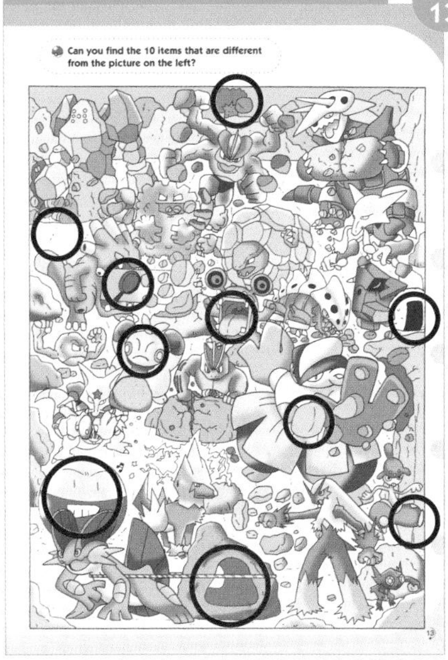

Can you find the 10 items that are different from the picture on the left?

Evolution Maze

Page 14

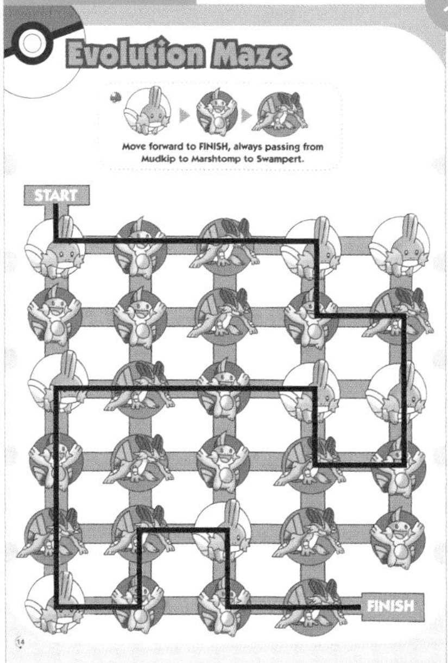

Evolution Maze
Move forward to FINISH, always passing from Mudkip to Marshtomp to Swampert.
START
FINISH

Find Wrong Evolutions

Page 15

Answer: 7 and 12. In 7, the third one, Psyduck, is wrong. In 12, the second one, Kingdra, is wrong.

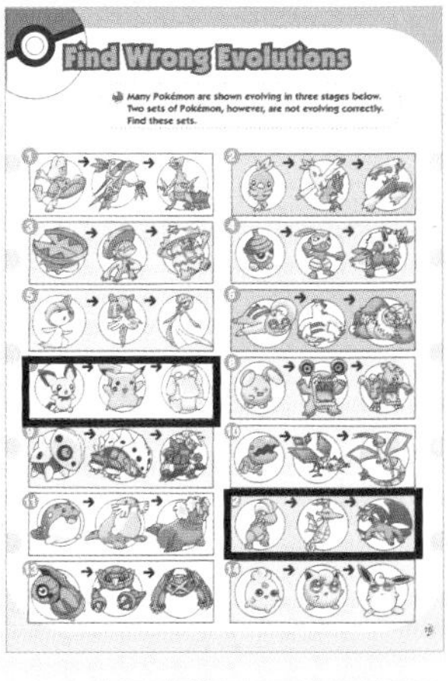

Find Wrong Evolutions

These are the correct evolutions:

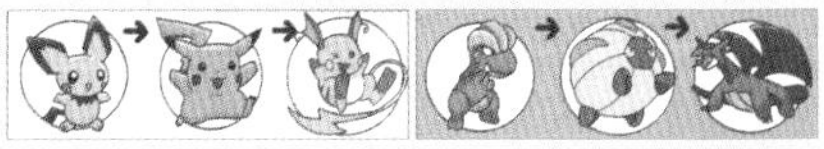

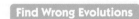

Silhouette Puzzle

Pages 16–17

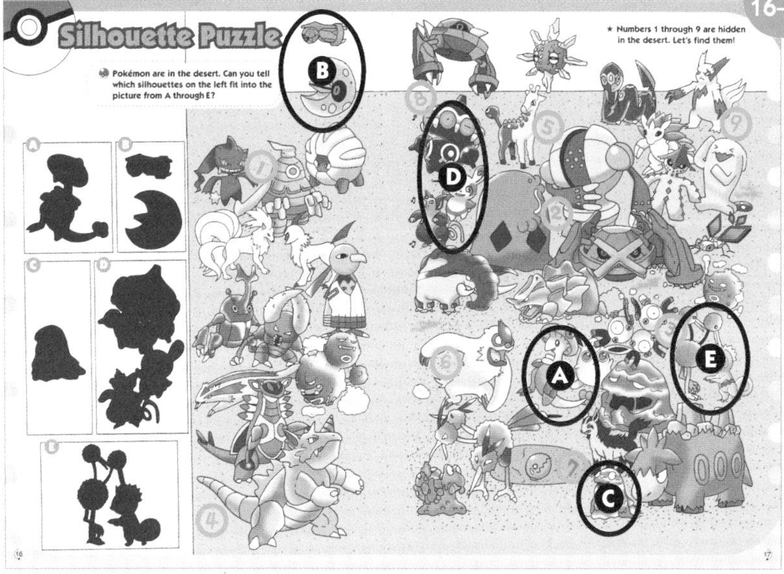

Silhouette Puzzle
Pokémon are in the desert. Can you tell which silhouettes on the left fit into the picture from A through E?
Numbers 1 through 9 are hidden in the desert. Let's find them!

The hidden numbers are circled in yellow.

Eyes Maze

Page 18

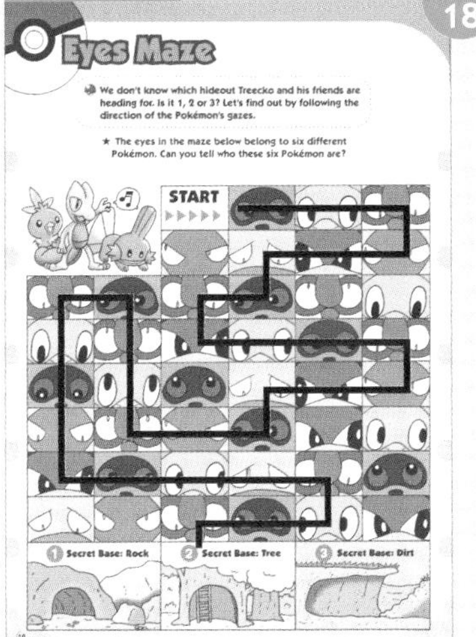

Eyes Maze
START
Secret Base: Rock
Secret Base: Tree
Secret Base: Dirt

The eyes in the puzzle belong to Vigoroth, Shelgon, Ludicolo, Zigzagoon, Taillow and Lombre.

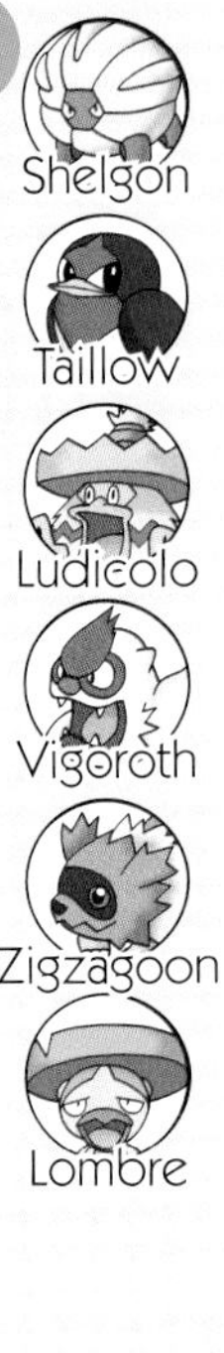

Shelgon
Taillow
Ludicolo
Vigoroth
Zigzagoon
Lombre